THE SEN

C.H.B. (CLIFFORD HENRY BENN) KITCHIN was born in Yorkshire in 1895. He attended Exeter College, Oxford, and published his first book, a collection of poems, in 1919. His first novel, *Streamers Waving*, appeared in 1925, and he scored his first success with the crime novel *Death of My Aunt* (1929), which has been frequently reprinted and translated into a number of foreign languages.

Kitchin was a man of many interests and talents, being called to the bar in 1924 and later amassing a small fortune in the stock market. He was also, at various times, a farmer and a schoolmaster, and his many talents included playing the piano, chess, and bridge. He was also an avid collector of antiques and *objets d'art*.

Kitchin was a lifelong friend of L.P. Hartley, with whose works Kitchin's were often compared, and was also a friend and mentor to Francis King, who later acted as Kitchin's literary executor. Some of Kitchin's finest works appeared towards the end of his life, including *Ten Pollitt Place* (1957) and *The Book of Life* (1960), but though they earned critical acclaim, Kitchin was bitterly disappointed at their lack of success with the reading public. Kitchin, who was gay, lived with his partner Clive Preen, an accountant, from 1930 until Preen's death in 1944. C.H.B. Kitchin died in 1967.

By C.H.B. Kitchin

Curtains (1919) (poetry)

Winged Victory (1921) (poetry)

Streamers Waving (1925)

Mr. Balcony (1927)

Death of My Aunt (1929)

The Sensitive One (1931)*

Crime at Christmas (1934)

Olive E. (1937)

Birthday Party (1938)*

Death of His Uncle (1939)

The Cornish Fox: A Detective Story (1949)

The Auction Sale (1949)

Jumping Joan, and Other Stories (1954)

The Secret River (1956)

Ten Pollitt Place (1957)*

The Book of Life (1960)*

A Short Walk in Williams Park (1971)*

* Available from Valancourt Books

THE SENSITIVE ONE

by
C.H.B. KITCHIN

With a new introduction by
DAVID ROBINSON

VALANCOURT BOOKS

The Sensitive One by C.H.B. Kitchin
First published London: Hogarth Press, 1931
First Valancourt Books edition 2014

Copyright © 1931 by C.H.B. Kitchin
Introduction © 2014 by David Robinson

Published by Valancourt Books, Richmond, Virginia
Publisher & Editor: JAMES D. JENKINS
20th Century Series Editor: SIMON STERN, University of Toronto
http://www.valancourtbooks.com

All Valancourt Books publications are printed on acid free paper that meets all ANSI standards for archival quality paper.

ISBN 978-1-941147-20-7 (trade paperback)
Also available as an electronic book.

Cover by M.S. Corley/mscorley.com
Set in Dante MT 11/13.9

INTRODUCTION

C.H.B. Kitchin's *The Sensitive One*, published in London in 1931 by Leonard and Virginia Woolf's Hogarth Press, is a strange novel. An odd novel. *Queer*, its original readers might have said. With an unobtrusively skillful and assured narrative voice, depicting a cast of mostly wealthy, upper-middle-class English characters inhabiting an upper-middle-class English world, *The Sensitive One* might come across as conventional, even old-fashioned. Yet it is crammed full of death, illness, violence, cruelty, and sex (or, at least, sexual desire) in the past and present, alluded to and depicted.

It's also a confusing novel. Not so confusing, perhaps, as other more self-consciously experimental texts of the period—the interwar years—with which it bears strong, if not always obvious, affinities. Novels such as Kitchin's own *Mr. Balcony* (1927), "a disquietingly mysterious and innovative work," as Francis King aptly put it.[1] Compared with *Mr. Balcony*, or with Ronald Firbank's campy, brilliant, deceptively insubstantial concoctions, which influenced both *Mr. Balcony* and Kitchin's first novel, *Streamers Waving*; or Woolf's *The Waves*, published the same year as *The Sensitive One*; or the works of Ivy Compton-Burnett, which, like *The Sensitive One*, expose the corrosive dynamics of middle-class English family life—compared with such novels, *The Sensitive One* is quite straightforward.

It begins in as orderly a fashion as one could wish: a table of contents listing the novel's twelve chapters, each designated simply by a month of the year, in chronological order. Next, a genealogical note, beginning "Mr. Moxhay had had seven children" and then identifying each of those children: "Archibald, who managed the family business," "Stuart, a clergyman," and so on. If anything, this initial orderliness seems excessive, reliant on heavy-handed structural conventions that modernism had already discredited and subverted.

But confusion quickly sets in, as the genealogical note lists the spouses and offspring of each of Mr. Moxhay's seven children. With

v

over thirty individuals spread across three generations, including some who share the same name and must be distinguished by diminutives (*Jenny* for the younger *Eugenia*; *Maggie* for the younger *Margaret*; etc.), the large Moxhay family—and the genealogical note that inventories its members—is overwhelming.

Still, at least the note situates the Moxhays in a comprehensible, ordered set of relationships. Immediately afterward, the novel's first chapter ("December") plunges the reader into a disorienting succession of names and relationships, attitudes and actions, as we meet the Moxhays in person, gathered joylessly for Christmas. Reading the first paragraph, and the pages that follow, I couldn't help but flip back repeatedly to the genealogical note, wondering, Who is Archibald Moxhay again? And Jenny Clark? And Stuart, Winifred, Perella, Hector, Phoebe, Cyril, John, and so on? Must I memorize this family's genealogy? But if we notice that the patriarch himself, the elder Mr. Moxhay, is just as confused about the family's cast of characters (his son Hector gives him a cheat sheet of the grandchildren's names and ages), we realize that this familial confusion is not an error, but rather an intended effect and central theme of the novel.

For *The Sensitive One* is very much about family, about families as places of repression—fueled by greed, controlled by tyrants and their collaborators—and the struggle to resist and escape this tyranny, to grow up and be oneself. Its plot centers on Margaret, the sensitive one of the novel's title, thirty-six years old and unmarried. Will she continue to sacrifice herself to her father's selfishness and her sister's mental illness? Or will she break free and make a bid for her own happiness? But Margaret doesn't believe she deserves happiness. Guilt over an act of violence she committed against her sister Euphemia when they were children—an act she believes, with a child's reasoning, caused Euphemia's mental illness—has formed the core of Margaret's identity. She has committed herself to a life of renunciation.

In this, she is like the eponymous protagonist of Kitchin's previous novel, *Mr. Balcony*, who "conceived the idea of altering [his] character, of doing violence to [himself], and being all that nature had not intended [him] to be, and nothing that she had."[2] Mr. Balcony's reason, unstated but implied, is his homosexuality—or rather, the miserable, humiliating life that awaits a homosexual in a deeply homophobic society.

Kitchin himself saw and lived more possibilities as a homosexual man in a deeply homophobic society than he allowed his creation Mr. Balcony to conceive of. Kitchin's wealth gave him greater freedom than most, as did his acceptance in artistic and social circles in which one could live an active and only partially closeted gay or bisexual life. In his case, that life included at least two long-term lovers. The first, Clive Preen, was an accountant with whom Kitchin lived for fourteen years, until Clive's sudden death in 1944. Their relationship, according to Francis King, was "blissful."³ Kitchin's second lover, George, was married and closeted, but lived with Kitchin on weekends for a number of years. In other words, Kitchin possessed a measure of freedom to live as a homosexual man.

Yet that freedom was decidedly circumscribed. As Francis King recalls, "Like [L. P.] Hartley, Kitchin was the sort of old-fashioned homosexual who was punctilious in concealing his proclivities at that period when to reveal them might well lead to blackmail or a prison sentence." The suffering this entailed could be profound. As King recounts:

> [Kitchin and Preen] were sharing a double bedroom at the best hotel in Liverpool, the Adelphi, when Preen suffered a massive heart attack and died. Kitchin realised that he must not give any indication of the intensity of his shock, horror and grief, for fear that the hotel staff and the ambulance men might conclude, rightly, that the couple were sharing a bedroom for some reason other than the desire for companionship or the wish to save money.⁴

Kitchin continued to practice this necessary concealment, this closeting, after Preen's death, as in the dedication to his 1949 novel, *The Cornish Fox*:

To the Memory of
CLIVE PREEN
who would have helped me with this story

Only readers who knew the essential facts of Kitchin's love life would have registered the intense poignancy of this understated tribute.⁵ And yet one needn't have been privy to such biographical details to recognize, from Kitchin's fiction, that he understood the potentially violent, even deadly repercussions of resisting his society's socio-sexual order. That understanding is the driving force behind, and very much the point of, *Mr. Balcony.*

The Sensitive One, too, alludes to homosexuality and homophobia, most notably in reference to Hector's musical son John, who has been expelled from school because of an unnamed but unmistakably homosexual scandal, and is planning to follow the example of his music tutor by converting to Roman Catholicism. In the opening chapter, the passage in which the news of John's expulsion is discreetly communicated (by Hector to Margaret, by Stuart to Archibald and Cyril, by Kitchin to us) is a miniature tour de force, both exemplifying and critiquing how discussion of homosexuality was confined, in middle-class circles, to innuendo, insinuation, and ellipsis. Within the space of two pages, and without anyone naming the issue at hand, Kitchin's characters display a multitude of models for understanding homosexuality (as cause for expulsion; as loathsome or pitiful sin; as criminal behavior in need of reform; as part of boys' school life; as object of medical or psychological inquiry; as a private matter; as a subject to be overlooked; as a subject to be concealed) and a range of responses, from Hector's professed unconcern and his care not to "bother" John about the matter, to Margaret's sympathetic concern ("What will he do?"), to Archibald's wish to conceal the scandal from the elder Mr. Moxhay, lest the knowledge kill him, to his son-in-law Cyril's attempt to introduce a medical, scientific perspective ("Dr. Leuwengrad, the great brain man, says——"), to clergyman Stuart's condemnation ("Very horrible. Very sad. Loathsome. . . . Case, I should think, for a reformatory") and transparently self-serving desire to expose his nephew's supposed moral turpitude, lest the wealthy and ailing Mr. Moxhay be "hoodwinked."

But *The Sensitive One's* societal critique extends even further. The novel delineates and indicts the violence perpetrated by conventional society on "the sensitive," those who resist the tyranny of conventional values: women, homosexuals, the queer.

Not that Kitchin romanticizes queerness. The novel's queerest character is Margaret's sister, Euphemia, whose name could not be more apt: she is almost an embodiment of euphemism, of the psychological and spiritual damage caused by a society that considers sexual desire impolite at best and unspeakable at worst. Euphemia's cold, beautiful exterior conceals an inner cauldron of sexual obsession, sexual frustration, and violent sexual rage.

Hector, Margaret's favorite sibling, is queer in a different, more positive way. Although the text provides occasional, ambiguous intimations that he might be homosexual, Hector's queerness consists in his independence from the rest of the family. While not seeking confrontation, he is the only one of the children to defy their father, steadfastly refusing to curry favor and toe the line. Hector is also the only member of the family to urge Margaret to live her own life. "Be discontented," he counsels her. "Remind yourself twenty times a day, how you, an intelligent and attractive woman of thirty-six, are squandering your life in an uncomfortable house, full of selfish half-wits and overpaid servants, deprived of friends, all reasonable interests, and even reasonable affection. Make plans for your own future, and be hard."

But for most of the novel, Margaret is unable to follow this advice. Convinced of her duty and her guilt, "the sensitive one" sacrifices herself to her tyrannical, abusive, monstrously selfish father and her secretive, disturbed, unloving sister. As in *Mr. Balcony*, in *The Sensitive One* Kitchin dramatizes not just the damage inflicted on the sensitive by a repressive society, but the way a repressive society causes strong sensitive people to internalize society's strictures and do psychic damage to themselves.

And then the novel goes further. Much further. By the end, this apparently old-fashioned, formally and stylistically conventional novel undoes the fundamental narrative scripts that make most novels intelligible. (Spoiler alert: I am about to give away key parts of the novel's ending. Readers might want to set aside this introduction now, and return to it after finishing the novel.)

The book ends on a poetic, symbolic, meta-narrative note, with Margaret and Hector walking off together in the fog, into the unknown:

They walked round the square, turned into Pont Street, and then out of it. It was like a walk in a dream, noiseless and effortless and of immeasurable distance. The fog grew thick again and swirled round them, so that unconsciously they would often pause and feel for the next step.

"Margaret."

"Yes."

"I thought I had lost you. Give me your hand."

"Here it is."

"What shall we do?"

"When? Now—or later?"

"Now. Shall we go back?"

"Are you tired?"

"No. Are you?"

"Not at all."

"What did you mean when you said, 'Now, or later?'"

"I wondered for a minute where you would want to go—in a day or two—to-morrow—any time."

"Where can we go?"

"Anywhere, except to the Poles. Africa, or the South Seas, or Littlehampton."

"And leave all this behind—and build things up—on the old foundations again?"

"The old foundations are buried. We are being born now. The world is waiting for us, like a piece of blank paper, on which we can write as we choose."

They walked on a long way in silence.

"Margaret, do you know where we are?"

"No—but it doesn't matter."

Margaret and Hector, and the novel they inhabit, have escaped, overthrown, subverted all traditional plots. The son has killed the father, but has not supplanted him. The daughter has refused the suitor her father tried to force on her, but has not chosen another. Or rather, she has chosen her brother, and he has chosen her. They complement one another: Margaret needed Hector to stand up to their father and free her from his control. And then Hector needed Margaret's long-prepared strength and courage to heal him from the shattering ordeal. Together, they have achieved liberation.

Kitchin prefigures this ending at the very beginning of *The Sensitive One*. The first chapter opens with a passage from a book

Archibald has idly picked up and quickly puts back down, a book we learn belongs to Margaret. Positioned like an epigraph to the chapter, it reads:

> *"But, in this turmoil, we shall have no part. At peace with ourselves, we shall be at peace with the whole world. We shall wait in silence and unselfishness for that event which is to be our destiny. As those who would snatch the bliss of love before due season may not afterwards enjoy the perfect fruit, so they who seek to hurry the spirit in its utterance shall never hear its full message. Life is, for us, the pathway to an ecstasy, the road on which all dreams shall be fulfilled."*

Like a leitmotif, the warning and promise of this passage reverberate throughout *The Sensitive One*, as characters pick up this same book-within-a-book and read a different, but related passage:

> *"which becomes faith. Lay not therefore too hard a hold on these external things. For as no flame (save the true flame) can burn without destroying, so these things may not enter into your life without impairing it, corroding the veins through which the truth shall flow one day.*
> *"O Joy conceived in darkness and struggling to be born!*
> *"O Joy . . ."*

At the end of the novel, just before Hector does battle with his father, and Margaret steps into her strength and selfhood, we finally learn the title of this book: *The Conflict of the Soul*.

In the end, Kitchin tells a tale of queer love—love between the sensitive ones, the strong queer siblings—who together overthrow the old, repressive, soul-crushing familial order and walk off into a fog of unknown possibilities on an unknown path, beyond the currently narratable, into a world that has not yet been charted, beyond the heterosexual romantic couple and marriage, beyond the patriarchal family.

More than a decade later, Kitchin's friend and fellow novelist L. P. Hartley, to whom *The Sensitive One* is dedicated (along with Alan Harris), would write his own tale of queer sibling love, the *Eustace and Hilda* trilogy (1944-47). But unlike *Eustace and Hilda*, Kitchin's queer sibling love story ends happily, or at least hopefully. "The End" of *The Sensitive One* is a beginning, with its queer heroes poised on the brink of a new world, ready to write a story that has never before been written.

DAVID ROBINSON
San Francisco

May 18, 2014

DAVID ROBINSON taught English Literature and LGBT Studies at the University of Arizona, where he attained the rank of associate professor. He left in 2011 to escape the desert heat. He has also been, at various times, an AIDS activist, a modern dancer, a grassroots urban-planning advocate, and a nonprofit director working for LGBT inclusion in Jewish life. In addition to several articles—including his favorite, "Pleasant Conversation in the Seraglio: Lesbianism, Platonic Love, and Cavendish's Blazing World"—he is the author of *Closeted Writing and Lesbian and Gay Literature: Classical, Early Modern, Eighteenth-Century*, published by Ashgate in 2006. He is passionate about undeservedly forgotten LGBT literature, the older the better. He is thrilled to be joining the faculty of College Preparatory School in Oakland as a high school English teacher.

NOTES

1 Francis King, "Foreword" to C.H.B. Kitchin, *The Book of Life* (Richmond: Valancourt Books, 2014) ix.
2 C.H.B. Kitchin, *Mr. Balcony* (London: Hogarth Press, 1989) 62.
3 King, "Foreword" to Kitchin, *The Book of Life*, vi.
4 King, "Foreword" to Kitchin, *The Book of Life*, vi-vii.
5 Kitchin, *The Cornish Fox* (London: Secker & Warburg, 1949).

THE SENSITIVE ONE

TO
ALAN HARRIS
AND
LESLIE HARTLEY

CONTENTS

		PAGE
I.	December	5
II.	January	18
III.	February	29
IV.	March	37
V.	April	43
VI.	May	49
VII.	June	58
VIII.	July	66
IX.	August	70
X.	September	82
XI.	October	92
XII.	November	101

GENEALOGICAL NOTE

MR. MOXHAY had had seven children:

Archibald, who managed the family business,
Stuart, a clergyman,
Hector, who had no profession,
David, who died as a baby,
Mortimer, who died suddenly at the age of 38,
Margaret, and
Euphemia, at whose birth Mrs. Moxhay had died.

Archibald's wife was named Eugenia. They had three daughters, Eugenia the younger (known as Jenny), Phoebe and Pearl, and Archie, a boy of 18. Jenny had married Cyril Clark, and they had one daughter Janet.

Stuart and his wife, Winifred, had eight children, Eric, Winifred (Winnie), Virginia, David, Arthur, Rachel, Paul and Ambrosia. Eric was the same age as Archie. The whole family lived together at a suburban vicarage.

Hector had married Rosa, the daughter of a peer. His children were John, aged 16, Rosamund and Margaret (Maggie).

Mortimer's young wife, Perella, had a baby named Opal, the same age as little Janet Clark.

Margaret and Euphemia were unmarried and lived with their father in Adelaide Square.

I

DECEMBER

"But, in this turmoil, we shall have no part. At peace with ourselves, we shall be at peace with the whole world. We shall wait in silence and unselfishness for that event which is to be our destiny. As those who would snatch the bliss of love before due season may not afterwards enjoy the perfect fruit, so they who seek to hurry the spirit in its utterance shall never hear its full message. Life is, for us, the pathway to an ecstasy, the road on which all dreams shall be fulfilled."

ARCHIBALD MOXHAY put the book face downwards, as he had found it, on a remote green plush settee. His eldest daughter, Jenny Clark, replaced the poker on its stand, while her uncle, the Reverend Stuart Moxhay, took up the warm position from which she had for a moment ousted him. Stuart's wife, Winifred, picked up a sprig of holly which had fallen from the top of a picture of the Grand Canal. Perella caught her profile in a long tarnished mirror, and frowned. Hector counted the number of persons in the room. His total came to nine; but he had forgotten to include himself, and had not noticed Archibald's second daughter, Phoebe, who was talking to Eric in an alcove. Mrs. Archibald Moxhay was helping her son-in-law, Cyril Clark, to find in the music-cabinet a song which he had sung with great success three years before, when he had just become engaged to Jenny. John Moxhay, the common ancestor of all the Moxhays present, sat on a sofa oblique to the second fireplace. He wore a quilted robe of red silk and his knees were wrapped in a tartan rug. His neck and the lower part of his face were covered with white and wiry hair. His younger daughter, Euphemia, shared the sofa with him and balanced on her lap a solitaire board, round the rim of which a single glass marble ran jerkily up and down. Mr. Moxhay suddenly stretched forth a hand, picked up the marble and dropped it on the floor. It rolled across the parquet underneath the piano.

"A year ago, dear Mortimer was with us."

Mr. Moxhay, who for ten years had been completely deaf, spoke slowly and with great loudness. All conversation ceased.

"A year ago"—he repeated. "Pearl, come here."

Perella, baptized Pearl but thus rechristened by herself, got up from her chair and approached the sofa.

"Sit down."

She sat on the arm.

"A year ago, I was saying, poor Mortimer was here."

He wiped his eyes with the back of his hand, and laid it gently on her shoulder.

"He was a good husband to you, Pearl?"

She wriggled slightly so that his hand fell on her knee. Then she produced from among the cushions a slate, to which a little sponge and a slate-pencil were attached. On the slate, clenching her teeth as the pencil squeaked, she wrote in untidy capital letters:

"HE WAS."

Mr. Moxhay made a humming noise for thirty seconds. Then he said, "And little Pearl, is she well? Is she here to-day?"

"YOU MEAN OPAL. YES. SHE'LL COME IN WITH THE OTHERS IN A FEW MINUTES."

"The fire needs looking to, I think."

While the words were still reverberating, Mrs. Clark darted across the room and stoked up.

"Good girl. A good daughter you've got, Jenny."

Mrs. Archibald bowed and smiled from the music-cabinet. Archibald, who preferred that his wife's name, when shortened, should be pronounced Gaynia, pursed his lips. Mrs. Clark, her task ended, took the slate from Perella.

"I LOVE MAKING FIRES."

"A most utilitarian accomplishment."

Stuart Moxhay took a piece of foolscap from his pocket and looked across the room at his wife who was standing by a window curtained with green velvet.

"Surely," he said in a needless undertone, "it's almost time."

Winifred nodded. Stuart and Archibald looked at their watches, Hector at the clock.

Mrs. Clark proffered the slate.

"I DO SO LOVE YOUR CHRISTMAS PRESENT."

"Very nice. I'm glad to hear it."

Perella rose.

"Don't go, Aunt Perella. There's lots of room."

Perella smiled, and went to the piano, and still standing, struck a few chords.

"How COLD IT IS OUTSIDE, TO-DAY!"

"Most seasonable weather."

"YES, VERY."

Mrs. Clark squeezed the last word in the bottom corner, and then, with the almost dry sponge, tried to rub out the conversation.

There was a sound of feet on the landing, and all except Mr. Moxhay looked up expectantly. The door opened and Margaret Moxhay, in one of her vaguely "period" gowns which had caused Perella to say at a smart tea-party, "One can see that she has made the grand renunciation", led into the room ten young persons. Of these, eight advanced in single file, linked together by chains of paper roses. The other two, little Opal Moxhay and little Janet Clark, were carried by their nurses.

"A good day to you, children. Pretty, very pretty."

Winifred, who had conceived the festoons, blushed with joy. During a moment's pause, some of the children expressed their compliments in pantomime. Margaret went to a writing-table and brought forward a tray covered with small paper parcels. She gave one to her father and said, "Pearl!"

Archibald came forward uncertain whether to conduct his youngest daughter in person. While he hesitated, she hesitated, but advanced at a gesture from Margaret, kissed the old man on the cheek, and took the slate from her sister.

"A VERY MERRY CHRISTMAS, GRAND-DADDY!"

"Thank you, thank you, my dear. And here's a little gift which I hope you will not spend all at once."

He pressed the packet into the palm of her hand. It was understood that one might convey thanks by another kiss, a curtsy and a smile.

"Winnie!"

Stuart hastened to the sofa, and spread out a list of his children on his father's knee. It ran as follows:

"ERIC STUART, AGED 18, WHO HAS ALREADY GREETED YOU TO-DAY.
WINIFRED MABEL (WINNIE), AGED 16.
VIRGINIA (WINNIE'S TWIN SISTER).
DAVID, AGED 15.
ARTHUR, AGED 14.
RACHEL, AGED 13.
PAUL, AGED 11.
AMBROSIA, AGED 9."

As each child approached Mr. Moxhay, Stuart pointed to the appropriate name on the list, and also announced it in a very loud voice; for he still believed that Mr. Moxhay might, some day, recover his hearing. With God, all things are possible.

"Bravo, Stuart," said Mr. Moxhay, presenting the packets as they were given to him, "a fine brood! You've beaten me, my boy. And I had six."

He had, indeed, had seven, but David, born two years after Mortimer, had died as a baby and was wellnigh forgotten.

Archibald went back to the green plush settee, picked up the book which lay there face-downwards, shut it and opened it. He found himself reading page 103, the last page of a chapter:

"which becomes faith. Lay not therefore too hard a hold on these external things. For as no flame (save the true flame) can burn without destroying, so these things may not enter into your life without impairing it, corroding the veins through which the truth shall flow one day.

"O Joy conceived in darkness and struggling to be born!

"O Joy . . ."

"Is that your book, Euphemia?"

"No."

"Yours, Margaret?"

"Yes."

At the post of duty, she did not turn her head.

"Who wrote it?"

"Giulio di Furore."

"Oh!"

He looked at the back of the binding.

"It says, 'Shamus O'Geoghegan'."

"Oh!"

He put the book down, took an old envelope from his pocket and began to make some calculations in pencil.

"Now, nurse."

Opal and Janet were in turn brought forward, and withdrawn clutching packets in their tiny hands. Perella and Mr. and Mrs. Clark approached the sofa and nodded as Mr. Moxhay smiled at their babies.

"You look more of a baby even than your child," he said to Mrs. Clark.

Mr. and Mrs. Clark nodded and smiled.

"You're a lucky girl, and Cyril's a good boy. Doesn't waste his time skating like your brother Archie."

Archibald, hearing this mention of his son who was having a holiday in Switzerland, looked up apprehensively. After all, Cyril Clark was only a relation by marriage, however meritorious it had been of Jenny (the correct diminutive for Eugenia the younger) to marry him.

But another thought soon claimed the aged brain.

"Hector!"

Margaret signalled to the nurses to remove the babies, and, her task ended for the moment, went to the settee on which her book was lying, and sat down. Hector rose as she passed, and went over to his father.

"Hector! Where are your children to-day?"

"I TOLD YOU. JOHN IS VISITING FRIENDS. ROSAMUND AND MAGGIE ARE AT HAYBROOK HAVING 'FLU."

"John is visiting friends. What friends?"

"SOME PEOPLE CALLED CONSIDINE."

Winifred had guided the eight remaining children to the alcove, where, in the shelter of a wooden negress who supported a big palm, they unwrapped their packets. No surprise, however, was in store for them; for each well knew that the contents would be a shilling for every year of the recipient's age. The older generation (which included Eric) ceased to talk, and listened to the vocal half of the conversation between Hector and his father. Perella, an adept with the telephone, had little difficulty in supplying the written half.

"Who are these Considines?"

"NICE PEOPLE."

"Hm! I hope so. When will the boy be back?"

"IN FOUR DAYS."

"I hope he asked your permission to be away from you at Christmas."

"YES."

"Bring him to see me soon. I won't have him cutting loose from the family."

"YES."

"If that's all you have to say, you might as well nod your head, instead of scraping at the slate. I can see a nod as well as you can."

Hector nodded.

"I hope your daughters are getting over their ailments."

"ROSAMUND IS. I'M AFRAID MAGGIE IS STILL POORLY."

"Take care of that girl. Take good care of her."

Hector nodded, and on being questioned no further, walked away.

There was a pause.

"And now," suggested Stuart to the assembly, "what about the hymn?"

"The total ages of the persons in this room," said Archibald, looking up from the envelope on which he had been scribbling, "amount to five hundred and ninety-seven years."

"Are you sure you haven't underestimated mine?"

"I know it to a day, Perella."

"'O come, all ye faithful'. Winifred, will you be so kind?"
She sat at the piano. The others arranged themselves behind her in concentric semi-circles, the smallest in front. Mr. Moxhay's sofa was pulled to one side so that he might enjoy the sight. Margaret, who was semi-detached, looked down the rows of faces, noticing here and there a family resemblance, an unsuspected beauty or blemish. The four married men were in the back row, and as she turned her head she could see a line of moustaches (Archibald's pendent and grey, Hector's thick and ginger-brown, Cyril Clark's black and waxy at the ends) leading up to Stuart's immense clean-shaven face, while the strong necks and shoulders of her brothers rose out of the welter of women and made Cyril Clark seem stunted and undersized. Perella was the best-dressed of the women, and Winifred, owing to her poverty combined with a refusal to dress like a parson's wife, the worst. Eugenia (pronounced Gaynia) had a grand presence, and Euphemia a wayward beauty. Eugenia the younger (Jenny) and Phoebe were imitations of Perella. Pearl was the best of her generation, Stuart's children being, except perhaps for Ambrosia, uniformly plain.

"O come, all ye faithful."

"So the total ages," thought Margaret, "amount to five hundred and ninety-seven years. And in my generation and the next we number seventeen nincompoops, while as for relations by mar-riage——"

> "O come, let us adore Him,
> O come, let us adore Him,
> O come, let us adore Him,
> Christ the Lord."

"Thank you, Winifred."
"Thank you, Winifred."
"So kind of you."
"Euphemia!"
She went to the sofa, and with her help Mr. Moxhay rose to

his feet. Conversation ceased. The ranks made a right turn and confronted him.

"My children—my grandchildren—my great-granddaughter—"

"He forgets nurse has taken Janet away," Mrs. Clark whispered. "How pathetic."

"My dear children, grandchildren and great-granddaughter, on this auspicious occasion, I rise, an old man, destined soon for that land to which my dear son, Mortimer—my dear son, Mortimer, who was with us last year—my dear son——"

He stopped suddenly, gasped for breath, and howled rather than wept. With a bound, Perella flung her arms round his neck and with her red lips caressed his hairy cheeks. Margaret rang the bell. Watts, the male nurse, came in almost at once, and, supported by him and Euphemia, Mr. Moxhay went out. It was a difficult moment. Perella went to the piano-stool and sat down. The room was filled with whispers, till someone mentioned the children.

Eight young persons and three mothers went downstairs. Archibald, Stuart and Cyril Clark walked to the front window; Hector and Margaret to the window at the back. Phoebe and Eric sat down in the alcove.

"What is it, about John?" Margaret asked.

"He was expelled from school."

"Asked to leave?"

"No, expelled—two days before the end of term."

She sighed and touched his hand.

"Oh," he said, "I'm not bothered about it—or bothering him."

"What will he do?"

Hector shrugged his shoulders.

"Where is he, Hector?"

"At home."

Meanwhile, clutching the curtain as if to make sure that no eavesdropper lurked behind, Stuart was muttering:

"I suppose you have heard about Hector's boy?"

" 'Genia had a guarded letter from Rosa," Archibald answered, wishing that his son-in-law were not listening so intently.

"Very horrible. Very sad. Loathsome. . . . Case, I should think, for a reformatory."

"Hm! Of course, at school——"

"No palliation is possible, Archibald."

"I do not palliate."

"Dr. Leuwengrad," said Cyril Clark, "the great brain man, says——"

"Our father," Archibald interrupted, "must not hear of this."

"Yet it is wrong that he should be hoodwinked."

"It might kill him."

"Dr. Leuwengrad——"

"Please, Cyril. I am old-fashioned enough to set no store by the new psychology. How is our father to be kept in ignorance? Shall the whole family conspire for two years more—till the boy is at the normal age for leaving school—to live a lie?"

"I shall leave Hector to do his own explaining."

There was a knock at the door, and a housemaid, who had forgotten to doff a paper headdress with which she had just diverted the servants' hall, announced Mr. Archibald's car. Perella, turning round, gave a little giggle. The groups merged.

"Tell Mrs. Stuart Moxhay," Stuart said to the servant, "that Mr. Archibald's motor has come for us. You will find her in the dining-room."

"Yes, sir."

"Well, Perella—another Christmas almost over. . . ."

"I wonder Stemmis didn't notice it."

"Notice what, Aunt Perella?"

"Didn't you see, Phoebe? Dorothy came in wearing a paper cap."

Eric made as if to run out on the landing.

We hardly show to best advantage, thought Archibald, when all together like this.

"The car," he said, "will hold six of you quite comfortably."

"I'm sure it will. Eric! Eric, you will take Winnie, David and Arthur home by bus. See, here is the money for your fares."

Stuart gave his son half a crown.

Perella turned to Hector and inclined her head slightly to one side.

"Hector, I'm sure your club is on my way."

"My car's at Haybrook. But I'll ring up a taxi now."

"You won't mind Opal's nurse?"

"Oh, no."

"And one for us, Hector," said Archibald.

He had put his car at Stuart's disposal and Winifred was not there to thank him for his self-sacrifice.

"Three," said Cyril Clark, "if you don't mind."

"Well, Margaret, another year is almost over. If I can be of any assistance to you, let me know. Our father . . ."

He continued in an undertone.

Hector's voice was heard through the open door:

"—three taxis, one, two, three taxis, to 12 Adelaide Square. Twelve. The Pont Street end. Ad—el—aide. . . . Yes, now."

"Dr. Miard was completely reassuring."

"Auntie Margaret, do you think Auntie Euphemia has the cutting about the rock-garden that she said she cut out for me?"

"One moment, Phoebe," said Stuart, drawing Margaret aside.

"Of course," she said, "we can, if you like, take Dr. Frost's opinion. Archibald didn't think we need."

"But to-day—this extreme feebleness, this mixture of shrewdness and confusion, and the emotion. . . ."

"For the last three years," she said, "it has been much the same. If you had been here the whole time——"

"I hope so."

"Now, Phoebe. Oh, the cutting. I'll send it you to-morrow."

"Well, Phoebe, time is slipping by. Perhaps by next Christmas—who knows what news you may not have for us?"

Eric, he reflected, would only be nineteen even then. It was a pity the boy's fancy hadn't fastened on Pearl. And, of course, a marriage of cousins. Still, there are circumstances in which it is not undesirable.

"I'm going to put on my things," Perella called to Hector, and she went out, followed by Phoebe. The hall was filled with voices.

"Are you ready, Winifred? We mustn't keep Stemmis waiting in the cold and doing nothing."

"Just one moment, dear. Now, Rachel, where are your gloves?"

"Eric, you had better be starting."

"Yes, Father."

One by one, thought Margaret, the bees fly from the old hive.

"Eric, dear, be sure and not let Arthur sit in a draught."

"All right, Mother. Paul, leave that alone."

Hector looked round the drawing-room door.

"Hector!"

"Yes, Margaret."

He went towards the window where she was standing.

"Must you go with that woman?"

"Does it matter?"

"No."

"Good night."

He kissed her and went out. She went behind the curtain, holding it with one hand so that the light should not betray her, and looked through the window. Archibald's motor, containing Stuart, Winifred and half their children, started first. The Clarks and the nurse with Janet got into a taxi. As the driver wound up the engine, Eric, Winnie, David and Arthur crossed the road in front of the house and walked round the corner. The Clarks' taxi started, followed by another with Archibald, 'Genia, Phoebe and Pearl inside. She is keeping him waiting, Margaret thought, but at that moment Hector opened the door of the remaining taxi and Perella, wrapped in furs, darted from the porch and got in. Then the nurse got in with Opal, and last of all Hector, who slammed the door from the inside. The taxi moved off.

Margaret opened the windows, looked round the room, saw her book lying on the settee, picked it up, and turned off the lights.

On her way upstairs, she saw Euphemia coming out of her father's room.

"How is he?"

"All right. Quite all right."

"Where are you going?"

"To my room."

"Oh, Phemy——"

Though aware that she was intruding, Margaret followed her sister to a room built on to a projection at the back of the house.

"How cold it is here."

"I'll light the gas-fire."

"You ought to have the front spare-room."

"I like this one."

"Phemy, you know Hector's boy has been expelled."

"Oh."

"We had better not say anything to father."

"No."

"Or—let anybody tell him."

"Yes. It might upset him."

"And, if Stuart or anyone writes to him, and I'm not there when he gets the letter, you should say—that it's a mistake, and that you heard from Hector, who says that—it was only some rag at the school. Just high spirits, you know, and healthy fun. John was the ringleader. If Stuart says it was anything else, it isn't true."

"All right, Margaret."

"And tell me, of course, if father asks any questions, and what you said."

"Yes."

"You need a new globe."

"The one by the bed is new. I don't like too much light."

"Well——"

Euphemia looked at the floor. Margaret went out and shut the door. Euphemia heard her steps in the corridor and on the stairs. For two minutes she stood motionless, her head on one side, her right arm pointing to the door. Then, with a sudden purpose, she went to the door, locked it gently, turned out the light, went to the window, drew back the curtains, released the dark blue spring-blind, opened the window and sat down in a chair opposite. Over two low buildings she had a view of the side of a house running parallel with the wing in which her room was, but less lofty. There were three windows in the wall of the house, dimly visible in outline only. But in addition to these there was a big skylight sloping with the roof, and inadequately curtained, through which came a bright light revealing half the interior of the room. Though the room might well have been a studio, the man who sat on a low and broad sofa at right angles to the further wall, was not an artist. His face seen in profile was square-jawed, clean shaven, and of darker complexion than the gold-brown hair on which the direct rays of a standard lamp were falling. He had big shoulders and long legs, which sprawled over a footstool. His ankles were thin. In one of his hands he held a magazine; in the other, intermittently, a pipe. On a table beside him were a cut-glass whisky decanter, a siphon and a glass, half filled. The room seemed comfortable, like a club smoking-room, and, save to the privileged, inaccessible.

When the gong sounded for supper in the Moxhays' house, Euphemia was still by her window, while the man in the room opposite was still sitting, smoking and reading.

II

JANUARY

"It isn't that you're backward, or haven't common sense, or don't read the papers," said Perella. "But you are all somehow outside things. I often wonder what you talk about, when you're not talking to me. Poland, I suppose, and Archibald's old college, and Stuart's curates and the revised prayer-book, Jenny's difficulty in getting a good nurse for Janet, and the rabbits that ate Hector's lettuce."

Margaret, sitting with her back to the engine, said nothing.

"I don't mean," Perella continued, "that you're afraid of everything new, or disapprove. I remember dining with the Clarks one night. Rather a family party it was. They had proper cocktails. Some old fogy said the usual idiotic thing about injurious modern habits, and Archibald, who's really rather a dear, I think, said, 'Oh, all young people have cocktails before dinner. Of course, we don't.' That sums it up wonderfully. 'Of course, *we* don't.' But he wasn't a bit shocked. . . . My own life has been so different."

"Yes."

"To begin with, I had no brothers and sisters. A large family was something I'd only heard of in books. (All large families in books are horrible. Have you noticed?) And then, I'm partly French. Not really, of course. My mother had a French grandmother, and took after her a good deal. She had quite a salon, when I was a child. I still remember her sitting in a big gilt chair, *à la marquise*, and receiving very spruce, rather elderly, men, who kissed her hand. It really was like a scene in a play. Of course, mother was *absolutely* respectable. But there was an air of—how shall I put it?—gallantry and romance about our home. There was so much life, so much gaiety. There was nothing you couldn't say. It was a splendid house to be a child in. No 'Don't do this; do that.' And yet my mother was very simple. Not at all pretentious, you know."

"No."

"Again, I've always loved art. I had an uncle a novelist. Historical novels he wrote—about Mary Queen of Scots and Queen Christine of Sweden—and other people like that. A lot of artistic people used to come to the house. Quite Bohemian, some of them. It would never occur to any of you to want to be an artist, would it? Your father, though he is a dear, simply wouldn't stand it. I don't know what he'll say when he hears that Hector's boy wants to take up music. By the way, I know Simiac, the composer of the ballet, *Petits Pois*—little peas, you know. I wonder if he would be any use. I must mention it to Hector. Simiac really is somebody. He's written some awfully modern things. It's no use nowadays being taught by people who only know Bach and Beethoven. Though, I confess, I adore Mozart. . . .

"I wonder, though, where John gets his music from. Not from Rosa, I should think. She's an awfully good sort, but she only seems interested in the country and hunting and that sort of thing. And Hector isn't musical either. Of course, Hector's not really like Archibald or Stuart. I think my dear Mortimer was most like him. I remember Mortimer telling me that Hector was always regarded as the lucky one of the family. He wouldn't go into the business, would he, like Archibald and Mortimer? At any rate, he's done better for himself, in a way, inventing that battery. I suppose his partner had money, and left Hector a good deal of it. It certainly was a stroke of luck to come across an old man like that—a bachelor —or did he hate his wife? I don't expect your father really likes Hector's being independent, does he? Not that Hector's rich—as rich as Archibald will be some day. But I do think it's bad luck on those in the business to be tied down to a salary and not given any capital to speak of. Archibald must be nearly fifty. Of course, he has a good income, but when it comes like pocket-money it isn't quite the same. I'd rather have less and own it outright. And then, the death-duties. . . .

"I suppose they thought Hector lucky to get Rosa. He was certainly the only one to marry into the aristocracy. That kind of thing means nothing to me. I had an aunt who used to sleep with

Debrett. She underlined her ancestors in red ink. We all thought it very silly. . . .

"Well, they say misfortunes never come singly. It must have been a blow about John. And now, poor little Maggie. Just when they thought she'd got right over it, too. She was your godchild, wasn't she?"

"Yes."

"Rosamund, they say, is Rosa's favourite. Will there be many people there, do you think?"

"I don't know."

"Archibald, of course, and 'Genia, and Stuart; not Winifred. She's got too many children to look after. I shouldn't be surprised if the Clarks are there. They'd hardly send Phoebe or Pearl. Archie, perhaps, if he's back from Switzerland. I wonder we didn't see any of them on the platform. I *am* glad I met you. . . .

"One seems to take stock of oneself on railway journeys, doesn't one? I hate reading in the train. If I hadn't seen you in this carriage, I should probably have been brooding over myself, wondering what was in store for me and what I was making out of life. Sometimes I see myself as a pathetic little widow living for her child. Depressing, isn't it? I should love to know what you think about yourself."

"What I think about?"

"About yourself—what you really think of living in Adelaide Square with your father and Euphemia. Of course, you've plenty to do, but it must be awfully quiet. Euphemia keeps to herself a good deal, doesn't she—spends hours in her bedroom with a crystal or planchette? Of course, we all know that she's not—that she hasn't your brains, or even mine, for that matter. She's not as sensitive as you are. I always call you the sensitive one. She is an *angel*, though. I've never seen a more unselfish person. You're both unselfish. I wish I was. That's another way in which your family is so different to mine. We never mentioned morals or duty. I remember once when I'd been naughty and sulked by myself all the afternoon, all mother said to me at bedtime was, 'Mon enfant, you only live once. You have wasted a day'. There's a good deal in that, too."

"I am not unselfish, Perella."

"Oh, yes, you are."

"Don't think I was asking for a compliment——"

She broke off and looked at the floor. "Why did I say that," she wondered. "What is the use of talking about myself to this fool? After all, she's not so bad. I am an unpleasant listener. I must talk more. If she knew—but she does and feels it. She's braving it out with her flow. She'll have more to say about me than if I had talked. My glum face—even though it is a funeral——"

Meanwhile, Perella was watching her, and wondering if it was true that Margaret, when nine years old, had in a moment of fury seized Euphemia's hand and held it for a few seconds in the nursery fire. It was a family scandal, and even Mortimer had been reticent when questioned about the scars on Euphemia's fingers. Yet, Margaret—the sensitive one—was probably quite capable of it. A tiff between the angels. She nearly laughed.

"Have you been to Haybrook before?" Margaret asked.

"Oh, yes. Don't you remember? Don't you remember, last spring? It was the Thursday before—before Mortimer was taken ill. I always think he scratched his hand on some barbed wire in one of the hedges round Haybrook, though he said he did it at home. I don't like the place. I think it's unlucky. It makes me want to cross myself or touch wood."

"I didn't know you thought it was at Haybrook——"

"I said so at the time. Of course, it's a very beautiful place. I don't know, though, that Hector's very fond of it. They know all the people in the big houses, but I don't think he's very keen on that sort of thing. After all, a man can't really take to his wife's friends. Mortimer didn't to mine. That's why I seem to have lost touch with so many people in my old set. I didn't insist. I knew it would spoil things if I tried to keep up with them. You see, it was out of a sense of duty that I threw myself into the bosom of your family—even though I shall always be a bit of an outsider."

"That's the beginning of Hay Wood. Those beeches——"

"Are we nearly there?"

"Another five minutes. Ramshott Station is about three miles beyond the house."

Perella opened her bag and attended to her face.

"Have you stayed here?" she asked, pausing.

"Oh, yes."

("I should have said 'Yes', not 'Oh, yes'," Margaret thought.)

"It must be pretty quiet after a day or two. I suppose they play bridge. But Rosa doesn't play. And rather exclusive shabby little dances, to get their daughters off. And, of course, during the day, you talk agriculture with your tenants. Has Hector any tenants?"

"Oh, no. Haybrook's a very small place. Just an ordinary garden and a field or two. The previous owners must have sold off all the land."

"It's funny how I don't seem to remember it. You go down a rather curving lane into the village, don't you? And if you follow the lane past the house it takes you on to the hills. We started to walk that way, but my shoe hurt. I love hills and mountains. I don't think I've ever enjoyed myself as much as I did at Murren last winter. Always something to do. I hope we shall find a taxi. Of course, one couldn't write and ask them to order one."

"There's a place near the station where we shall be able to get one."

"Archibald will see to it. He must be on the train. Stuart too, I suppose, unless he went earlier to make arrangements. I think clergymen always enjoy funerals. I can imagine Stuart saying to Archibald, 'You pilot me through this world. I'll pilot you through the next'. Oh dear, I oughtn't to have said that. Don't repeat it, Margaret, on any account. You see, I wasn't brought up to be orthodox, and at times like this I'm afraid I become rather Voltairian. Not but what I'm very sorry for them all. It doesn't mean I don't feel it."

She wiped a tear, and was about to open her bag again, when the train stopped at Ramshott Station.

"Ouf! It's cold. There he is, Margaret. Archibald! Where's Stuart? Oh, I thought he would . . ."

They drove in a shaking and draughty car to the church.

Sitting in one of the front pews, Perella scanned the wreaths, hoping to identify the one which she had ordered. "These little ones," she thought, "can't have cost more than ten and six. Mine should be that one at the side, but I said I wouldn't have lily of the valley."

The organ played a gloomy voluntary, and the principal mourners, Hector, Rosa and John, took up their positions.

The Rector and Stuart divided the service between them.

"After all," thought Margaret, as they moved to the grave-side, "more terrible things have happened. More terrible things will happen. Had she lived, she might have had a wretched life—headaches, long fits of depression. . . . A delicate child—the sensitive one—surpassed the whole time by a livelier sister. . . . It isn't so very terrible."

She saw Hector make as if to take his wife's arm; the faint gesture with which he was repelled; John's quiver of uneasiness when Hector took his hand. Stuart looked bigger than ever and almost menacing. Perella was standing in a model attitude, as who should say, "I can behave as well as any of you on sacred occasions." A model attitude. Why not? How else should she stand? Archibald was blowing his nose. 'Genia hadn't come. Of course, her mother wasn't so well as they could wish. Archibald pressed his handkerchief into his sleeve clumsily, with gloved fingers. Rosa had a very bad cold. One funeral makes many. But apart from a swollen nose, she looked fat and well enough. After all, it wasn't so very terrible. . . .

Those must be village people, and those, too, inferior village people, gloating behind the yew-trees. A very Christmassy churchyard, cold and sombre in spite of the pale January sun. One funeral makes many. (The phrase was continuously beaten out as if by a little dream at the back of her mind.) "They are horrors which most people have to go through—some many times. After all, it isn't so very terrible. Had she lived, poor little thing. . . ."

She noticed John, lanky and unattractive, with a large pale face, standing on his father's left. "This," she thought, "is an agony for him—not because he is so terribly grieved, or appalled by—what was Stuart's phrase?—the seemingly purposeless taking of a young life—but because the occasion is to him so utterly dreary, so devoid of hope or promise of any good thing to come. He hates us, wretched youth; he hates our deaths and lives and lamentations. He longs for all the things which pass us by, adventure, romance, brilliance. He wanders about the gloomy country and lives on dreams—between meals. Poor thing, what will he do—with our weight on the top of him?"

She watched him and saw how he slipped his hand suddenly from his father's, pulled out a dirty white handkerchief and dabbed his eyes, while his large mouth was twisted into an ugly grin. Then he walked out of the churchyard, but before he had reached the gate burst into a loud and convulsive sobbing which smothered the elegant whimpering of the others.

"That's simply nerves," Perella murmured.

Margaret had an impulse to rush after him and take him in her arms, cover him with kisses, and say, "My dear, my dear, I understand." "But if I did," she thought, "he would never forgive me." And she waited by Perella's side till it was time for them to leave the churchyard.

" 'The seemingly purposeless taking of a young life'. That was a fine phrase, Stuart."

"I hold it hypocritical to belittle these afflictions."

"Margaret, you must eat something. There are some sardine sandwiches over there."

"Although it's cold, it's a mercy we had some sun. If it had been last week, we should all have been drenched. And you know, you have all my sympathy. And do take care of yourself, Rosa. You have a shocking cold."

"Her Ladyship's motor, Thompson, please."

"Oh, don't, please, trouble . . . all my sympathy, and good-bye."

"Archibald, when ought we to go?"

"In five minutes. The taxis are there. You'll come with Stuart and me, won't you?"

"Rosa," said Stuart, "I have already said how——"

Rosa pressed a handkerchief to her nose. "If you'll excuse me," she said, "I think I ought to go to bed at once. It's nothing but a bad cold, but still——. Hector, I'll see Dr. Moss this afternoon."

"I'll telephone."

"Good-bye, Margaret; good-bye, Perella—Stuart—Archibald—it was so very kind of you to come."

"Good-bye, Rosa—and our profoundest sympathy."

Archibald opened the door, and Rosa went upstairs.

"Now we must go, dear Hector. Oh, Hector, you know how I feel for you."

Perella embraced him and kissed him, as she had embraced and kissed Mr. Moxhay on Christmas Day.

Hector's clear pink-brown complexion reddened slightly.

"Hector," said Margaret in a half-whisper, "may I stay till a later train? Someone ought to be with Rosamund this afternoon."

"Oh, do——"

"Margaret."

"I'm staying till later, Archibald. Will you telephone to Euphemia?"

"Do you think you can leave our father so long?"

"Euphemia's there, Stuart."

"I know, but none the less——"

"Good-bye."

"Good-bye."

Hector shut the front door.

"Come in and sit down. Or would you like to lie down?"

"Where's Rosamund?"

"We've sent her over to the Talbots for the day."

"In that case——"

"No, you're not in the way at all. You might like to talk to John. He's probably locked himself in his bedroom, but he'll come down later."

"When is my train?"

"Four thirty-seven."

"Don't bother about me. I'll lie down here, on the sofa."

It was a large, uninteresting room. The chairs and sofa were covered with a blue-and-white cretonne, of which the curtains were also made. There was a deep cream paper on the walls. In the middle of the room a modern mahogany table supported a silver vase, two photographs (one of Rosamund and one of Lord Dumelerer, Rosa's father) and half a dozen books, of which four dealt with the management of horses. The *Graphic*, torn and two months old, lay on a settee. "The 'Home Beautiful'," Rosa had said once, "has never been much in our line. It's too suggestive of nitrates and oil for my taste." Well, as Perella had afterwards commented, if Rosa preferred the "Home Hideous", presumably she had a right to it.

Margaret lay down on the sofa and looked out of the window on to a square grass lawn bounded by silver birches, and suddenly, as a shaft of sunlight struck the foremost row of trunks, some quality of the trees, graceful, yet severe, filled her with calm. They satisfied a need which, when dispirited, she often felt for something bright and hard and cold. In the twinkling of an eye she had ceased to exist as it were on sufferance. It was, indeed, much the same sensation which she had when, still a child, she first heard the second movement of Beethoven's "Moonlight Sonata". Afterwards she had tried to perpetuate the mood by learning the piece, but the charm dwindled the more she sought to capture it, till in the end, whenever she thought of the melody, she had in mind two separate pieces of music—the magical phrase as she had first heard it, and the comparatively unimportant piece which later she had learnt to play.

She was still looking at the trees with pleasure, when John came into the room.

"I'm sorry, Aunt Margaret; I didn't know you were resting."

"I'm not. Do stay."

He walked moodily round the room, his hands in his pockets, and then said rudely:

"If you didn't want to rest, why did you stay after the others?"

"I thought——" she began, and then realised that the entertaining of Rosamund had only been a pretext. Yet she could not tell John that she had felt unable to travel back with Perella and Stuart. He might repeat it and make trouble.

"I wanted to see you," she said.

He sat down nervously.

"If you start talking about me, I shall go out for a walk," he said, and added angrily, "Father's going to get me a tutor."

"And what will he teach you?"

"Oh, all the silly things one has to learn, I suppose."

"What about your music?"

"I go to Kenrick, the organist at Ramshott, for that. But I want to go to London."

"In another three years——"

"But I shall be at Oxford then. Do you mind if I play something?"

She felt that she ought to stop him, but reflected that Rosa's trouble was only a bad cold, and that her room was not immediately over the drawing-room.

He went to the piano and played one of the fugues from Bach's *Kunst der Fuge*. He set no store by touch or use of pedal, and seemed to take pleasure in emphasising all the discords, which his mistakes increased in number.

"Did you like that?"

"Not as you played it."

The answer seemed to please him, and he began another and simpler fugue, taking more pains with it. When he was half-way through, the parlour-maid came in suddenly, nodded apologetically to Margaret and went up to the piano.

"Please, Master John, the mistress says will you kindly not play the piano any more to-day."

"All right."

He banged down the lid of the piano, and the maid went out.

"There, you see," he said, "what it is to live here."

"You're lucky to have a garden."

"You're right."

Without looking at her he opened the French window, crossed the lawn and disappeared among the birches.

Hector did not come in till Margaret had had a solitary tea. He walked with her to the station and seemed relieved when she made no reference either to the funeral or to John. It was a clear and cold evening.

"I'm afraid you may find fog in London."

If that were so, she thought, her father would have missed his drive. Euphemia would be tired, sitting with him all the afternoon.

"I oughtn't to have stayed," she murmured.

"I don't see why not," he said brutally. "None of us took any trouble about you."

"I was thinking more of Euphemia."

"My dear Margaret, think of yourself sometimes."

"I do—too much, far too much."

"Well, good night, dear."

He kissed her with affection.

"Good night, Hector—and come and see us soon."

He made a face, and waved as the train moved away.

III

FEBRUARY

MR. MOXHAY's motor-car went round the park for the last time at the speed of a carriage. It was an afternoon in late February. The air was soft and warm, and even Mr. Moxhay, who sat in the middle of the chief seat, wrapped in rugs, relaxed his vigilance and hardly troubled to comment or ask questions, as was his habit, on everything that he saw. Margaret, in a small space by his side, was glad to be left in peace. Though she had the slate on her knees, and the slate-pencil in her right hand, she had almost forgotten that it was the hour of the drive, and had abandoned herself to day-dreaming in a way that was seldom possible in her father's presence. There was about that fallacious foretaste of spring an enervating delicacy which produced a gentle turmoil of the senses. As she gave herself up to the enjoyment of its treacherous pleasure, she was reminded of similar days in her childhood when she had been taken out for the first walk after a bad cold. She remembered well her slow steps, the slight fatigue which the first exercise in convalescence had caused her, the feeling of warm dampness on the hands and in the small of the back, the indolent curiosity with which she had turned her gaze now to a branch, now to a crocus-bud, and above all the preciousness of the freedom that was hers again after too many dismal days in bed, wakeful nights, confinement in a hot nursery with screens and rugs and a dull brown quilted dressing-gown, which she had to wear if ever she went into the passage. At such times (and as she used to have at least one bad cold a year, they had not been infrequent), the recognition of her body's weakness had seemed to charm away all fretfulness of mind. Indeed, she used to look forward to one such day in every year, and when the fitful anniversary came round, the memory of her early happiness strengthened by a repetition of much the same physical elements, brought her a similar happiness again. This power to find serenity, and sometimes, as on first hearing the second movement of the "Moonlight Sonata", ecstasy, through the senses, atoned perhaps for her powerlessness to find it in thought or action. Hence her "unselfishness", of which, not without a contemptuous pity, her family made so much. Indeed, some saw in it little to be praised—a following of the line of least resistance, an easy sacrifice. Had her desires been strong, they would have been thwarted. The life in Adelaide Square did not encourage the intelligence or independent action of any kind. Thus Perella and Archibald's wife could say, "It is as well", while Stuart praised God's wisdom in having blessed the family with one so dutiful. But for this unselfishness there was yet another and less happy cause, which that very night was destined to recall.

"Margaret."

Her eyes were suddenly filled with alertness, her muscles stiffened with readiness to obey.

"Margaret, who are those people who—what's the name of the terrace behind the one where the Clarks had their first flat?"

"Do you mean Leslie Terrace or Sibylla Gardens?"

"Leslie Terrace, of course. Sibylla Gardens is on the right. You ought to know that by now. What's the name of those people we used to know who lived there?"

"I'm afraid I can't remember."

"Think, girl. Archibald brought them to dinner the night your sister had whooping-cough. A good-looking woman, with her hair done in a fantastical way."

"Measles. Colonel and Mrs. Ledder-Jones. But they lived in Hooper Road."

"Hooper Road. That's it, of course."

He mused for a few moments, as if it was the address and not the name of his guests that he had wished to remember. Margaret rubbed the conversation off the slate.

"Write down 'Hooper Road'."

"Hooper Road."

"You still make your P's like D's. You've written 'Hooder Road'. Write it again."

"Hooper Road."

"That's better. Why can't you always write like that? Your sister's writing is much better than yours. You can't expect my eyes to make out any scrawl. You must take more trouble with that hand-writing of yours. Well, I have enjoyed this drive, and I hope you have too."

"Very much, thank you."

"Remember, when I go upstairs, I want to see that balance-sheet."

"Which one?"

"The one that came yesterday, of course. The silk people."

"Courtaulds?"

"Yes, of course. You're very slow in the uptake to-day. Well, I have enjoyed this drive. I hope you have. Have you?"

"Very much, thank you."

It was ten o'clock, and Mr. Moxhay had long been put to bed. Margaret sat in the green plush drawing-room, reading and thinking and half-consciously listening to a long rattling sound ending with a metallic click, that was repeated every two or three minutes. When she raised her eyes, she saw her sister in a cheap blue evening-dress, sprawling on the sofa and playing with a roulette wheel.

"Who gave you that?" she asked.

"Archibald."

"For Christmas?"

"Yes."

"I haven't seen it before."

Then she read for ten minutes, though still thinking of the strange and solitary game.

"What an extraordinary present," she said at length.

"Why?"

"I suppose he thought it would be amusing to have it at parties. What are you doing?"

"Testing it."

"How?"

"I'm seeing if the numbers come up equally. I put them down on a piece of paper."

"But you will need several thousand spins for that to be of any use."

"I have spun it several thousand times."

"I haven't seen you."

"No; in my bedroom."

Margaret turned again to her book, and for half an hour made as if to read. At a sudden cry she looked up, and saw her sister raise her right hand with its three scarred fingers, and fling the ball on to the revolving wheel. There was a loud rattle and the ball jumped out and rolled across the floor.

"What's the matter?"

Euphemia glared at her with angry eyes.

"What's the matter, Phemy?"

"Nineteen's come up four times running. It's always ahead of the other numbers."

"I suppose the wheel isn't true."

"I hate nineteen."

"Why? Because it comes up so often?"

"No. It comes up because I hate it."

"That's nonsense."

"Very well. Seven and twenty-three and thirty-five come up almost as many times, and I hate them too. Eleven never comes up, nor one, nor seventeen. . . ."

"Do these numbers mean anything?"

"Yes; I want eleven to win."

"You're not really testing the wheel. You're having a competition between the numbers?"

"Yes."

"What do these numbers mean? What does eleven mean?"

Euphemia did not answer, but left the sofa and lying on the floor raked with her right hand underneath a china-cabinet where the ball had rolled.

"Shall I help you with the poker?"

"No, I've got it."

"Let me try throwing it."

"I've got a splinter in my finger."

Margaret examined the injury. It was in the fourth finger, the most deeply scarred of the three.

"Let me get it out for you."

"I can do it myself. I've got some tweezers in my room."

She picked up the roulette wheel, the ball, a piece of paper half-covered with figures, and a pencil and went to the door.

"Good night, Margaret."

"Good night. I wish you'd tell me what the numbers mean."

Euphemia shut the door and went upstairs.

Margaret took up her book and then laid it down. "I pushed her fingers in the fire," she thought, and then in order to slur over the memories of past self-torture, went on quickly, "After all, the young are always cruel. It's absurd to worry too much about what one did when young." "I kicked you myself," Hector had said, "I kicked you myself, on the ankle. You showed me the bruise." But the bruise vanished all too quickly. The marks of the burns remained. It had been difficult, though a comfort, to speak to Hector about it. "I am good for nothing," she had said, "I have really no right to be happy. Why should I try to please myself?" She remembered all the incoherence of the paroxysm. He had laughed and stroked her hair a little. "The young are always cruel. . . . I kicked you myself on the ankle. Do you suppose it has worried me? It was only about an hour after you gave me a diary, too; do you remember? That made it worse." "I wish you had broken my ankle," she said. "I wish you had lamed me for life. Kick it now—break it." "My poor Maggie, do you really feel you've committed a terrible sin, all those years ago?"

Now it was more than twice as many years ago. At the time of that very intimate conversation, Hector had been going up to Oxford for his first term. No doubt she had dared to speak to him because she would not be seeing him for eight weeks.

"Really, if things weighed with us like that. . . . When I remem-

ber the things I did to a boy at my preparatory school. . . . I'm
not responsible for what I did when I was twelve, nor are you for
what you did when you were eight." "But if we looked at things
that way, we should be wrong to hang people." "Perhaps we are.
But hanging isn't a matter of right or wrong. It's more like using a
fire-extinguisher." The conversation had wandered away from the
point. A few months afterwards he had asked her if she still worried about it, and she had said, "Not much".

This was not true, and she had never told him the whole truth.
She had not come to the real kernel of her worry till later, when
she and others had realised that Euphemia was ——. For this gap
there was no word that was not too painful to be used. Euphemia
was not as other people, though, as Perella said, "No doubt she was
as happy as most". If she was happy in her own way, why should
it trouble anyone? She was well able to look after Mr. Moxhay. She
was very pretty. But she was not as other people. Try as one would,
it was impossible not to be angry with her sometimes, and one's
terrible repentance afterwards was so indifferently received. "Were
you angry? I didn't know."

Once, and once only, Euphemia had run in tears to her room
and bolted the door, and by ill luck the same evening Margaret had
seen a paragraph in the paper that brought her all the enlighten-
ment of dismay. It was a gossipy article on psycho-analysis, with
the "complex" as its theme. Part of it she knew by heart. "Simi-
larly," it read, "shocks received in early childhood, even if involving
little or no permanent physical injury, have often been known to
produce in later life a mental deformity, sometimes amounting to
lunacy and resulting in the patient's premature death. There is a
case on record of a Maidstone girl who when four years old was
badly scratched on the face by a Persian cat. For many years she
appeared to be quite normal, and did not even suffer when a cat
was in the room, but when she was twenty-three . . ."

The day after, an eminent doctor had written an indignant letter
to the paper, protesting in the name of common sense that if the
substance of the article were true, half the children in England
would be half-wits, and suggesting three alternative explanations

for the case of the Maidstone girl. Margaret had read the letter without interest. The agonies of the intervening day and night had frozen her mind in a despair so deep as almost to be serene. It was no use, she had decided, asking a doctor about it. He would be sure to try to comfort her. It was no use speaking to Hector, of whom, now that he was married, she saw little.

"Henceforward," she wrote on a piece of note-paper, "I dedicate myself to others. I have no right to live for myself, or if I have such a right, I renounce it. Happiness may come to me in forgetting myself, but I shall train myself to ignore it. May I seek to see no happiness or comfort, except reflected in other people, ever again."

She had dated the paper and sealed it up in an envelope, on which she wrote, "Destroy unread. Margaret Moxhay". A few months afterwards she had destroyed it, thinking that in preserving the document she was gratifying a taste for melodrama. But the keeping of her resolution became such a habit that there were times when she could forget its origin for weeks on end. Euphemia, too, did not horrify her close observation by doing anything very terrible. It was only intermittently that some event, like the game with the roulette wheel, carried Margaret's thoughts back to what she could herself now call the soul-storm.

Tired of her thoughts, her paper and her book, she watched the fire, which was dying. Peak after peak of glowing coal became white and cindery. The vibrations of the barely visible flames passed over new chasms, leaving the old remote and lifeless. Each moment new secrets were revealed. The depths crumbled and little shooting stars dropped through the bars into the waste land below. The general brightness contracted, became a full-blown rose whose petals decayed at their tips. The centre ran to seed and fell two inches with a sudden little noise. The blight spread, dappling the red with tawny patches. There was a draught from the door, a draught along the floor, a draught from the windows where the thick curtains gaped and swayed. The electric lights seemed to lose their force, as if they too must die with the fire and could not withstand the invading chilliness, while the furniture grew more massive and jutted out further into the dwindling room, as if one were already stumbling against it in the dark. The clock prepared to strike.

Margaret went to the windows to see that they were bolted, put the guard in front of the fire, turned out the drawing-room lights, carried the vases of flowers down into the hall so that they should be revived by the fresher air, looked to the front door and two windows on the stairs. When she reached the third floor she walked quietly down the passage leading to Euphemia's room. She stood outside the door till she had heard four times the sound of the roulette ball rattling into the little metal groove.

IV

MARCH

PERELLA, from Cannes, wrote Margaret a long and interesting letter. A mass of ideas like an accumulation of half-empty matchboxes had littered her mind for some days, and it was a pleasure to make use of them. To tell half is to conceal half. The Moxhays, Perella reflected, did not approve of trips to the Continent. To go to Leipzig or Prague intent on obtaining contracts or investigating a new machine was no doubt permissible; but the Riviera needed excuse or apology.

"I am," she wrote, "more than half ashamed of being here. The sky is so radiantly blue, the sea so calm and ultramarine, and the flowers—how can I describe them? It seems in such a place absurd that there should be lady-companions. That is, in fact, what I am. Lady Maule, however, is kindness itself. She is, of course, an old friend of my mother's. . . ."

"I wish you could be here," she continued. "I can picture you, your large eyes watching the people with a rather scornful curiosity. Achille Rofflard, the tennis star, is in our hotel. He is a spruce dahlia of a man and has a little sweet-pea of a woman with him. My friend, Simiac, the composer of the ballet *Petits Pois*, is also here, but in another hotel. There was rather a scandal about him, because he—but I think I'd better not go into that, or you'll think we're a disreputable crew. Quite the contrary, I assure you.

"We have the most marvellous suite. I have a delightful bedroom facing the sea, with an enormous *cabinet de toilette* attached to it. The floor is a mosaic of Adam and Eve—very futurist of course. The shaving mirror has a little electric light let into the glass at the bottom. It almost makes me wish I were a man, and really needed it. I haven't seen them in England yet, have you?"

Of course, she hasn't, Perella thought. Margaret sees nothing till it's twenty years old, unless it's at the circulating library. And even there she doesn't see much!

"I hear"—(now she'll wonder who's been writing to me)—"that you're moving to Shoreston earlier than usual. Do you think you'll get Seamew again? I had an idea the people didn't want to let it till after Whitsun. I am most grieved to learn that your father hasn't been so well lately. Of course it's very difficult for him to get enough fresh air in London, and I think Dr. Miard is quite right in saying that the sea breezes will soon set him up."

At this point she lit a cigarette, and pondered for a few moments.

"I am writing to a friend of mine, Alexander Kithen, who lives with his mother in a village bearing the wonderful name of Clome Extrinseca, about twenty miles from Shoreston, to call on you. His mother was the old Lord Kithen's second wife. (It's pronounced 'Ki'en'.) The present Lord Kithen, Alec's half-brother, popularly known as Kitty, is a bad hat, divorced once, and bankrupt twice, I believe. Alec is quite different, rather literary and quite intelligent. He had a play produced once, called 'Why didn't She Do It?' I can't remember what it was she didn't do, let alone why. The play wasn't much of a success. But I think you'll like Alec. I never see him without thinking of Jane Austen's description of Mr. Elton in—oh, I can't remember which one—'a very pretty man'. He has a very silky little black moustache and a good 'country' complexion, not unlike Hector's, though sallower. He's been getting rather serious lately, and I think seeing you might enliven him."

"This is going too far," she thought, heavily erasing the last sentence. "And now for the good impression."

"Nurse sends me a little line about Opal every day, and says she is doing splendidly. It was so kind of you to have them to tea. Opal already *loves* her grandfather. He always took such an interest in poor Mortimer's baby. I long to be back and bring baby round myself. Perhaps we shall be able to find rooms at Shoreston for Easter, so as to be near you all. I shall feel so lonely in London without any of you there. Lady Maule is waiting for me to go to

the Casino with her, so I must stop now.—With love to you all.
Your ever affec.

"PERELLA."

The same post that brought Perella's letter to Adelaide Square
brought one from Stuart to Mr. Moxhay.

"MY DEAR FATHER—I was more than delighted yesterday afternoon to find you looking so well, and I applaud your decision to
follow Dr. Miard's advice and go to Shoreston as early as you can.
As you said, even if Seamew is not to let, Margaret can easily find
another suitable house from the agent. Perhaps, indeed, it is just
as well that you cannot go to Seamew, as the dust from the parade
cannot be beneficial to the throat.

"I have after much consideration decided to inform you of a
fact which I felt unable to communicate to you in your presence.
It concerns Hector's boy. I have waited till now to give you the
distressing tidings, not only because I hoped that Hector would see
fit to announce them to you himself, but also because I could not
bring myself to do an action which might be described as telling
tales about a brother. My conscience, however, can no longer
connive at your deception, and I have sufficient trust in your good
judgment to know that you will acquit me of any odious intentions.

"Hector's boy was expelled from school a week before the end
of last term—that is to say, about a fortnight before Christmas. He
spent Christmas at Haybrook. No doubt Hector was very properly
reluctant to bring him to our happy gathering in Adelaide Square.
The boy has since that time been loafing about at home, where no
doubt time lies heavily upon his idle hands. As far as I can learn,
Hector has only once attempted to find a tutor for the lad, and,
that attempt having for some reason ended in failure, has made
no further effort, but allows him to roam about by himself, and
read what he will. This, I need hardly say, I conceive to be no sort
of education either of intellect or character. It is true that the boy
has a leaning towards music, and receives, I understand, desul-

tory instruction from one, Kenrick, the organist at Ramshott. I have, however, inquired from my friend the Rector of Ramshott, and find that he has no great opinion of his organist either as a performer on the instrument or as a man.

"I am naturally anxious not only for the sake of the boy, but for the sake of his sister, Rosamund, who, though a charming and lively girl, is at an impressionable age, and susceptible, I should say, to evil influence. The boy, when I saw him at poor Maggie's funeral, struck me as being in grave need of discipline. I am convinced that if he is allowed another three months of this dangerous freedom he will become permanently unsuited not only for the business, in which I believe it was your intention to place him, but for any serious vocation.

"The reason for John's expulsion I must leave for Hector to tell you.

"I pray that this letter may give you as little pain as may be. Should you wish to consult me at any time, you have only to tell Margaret to telephone to the Vicarage.—I am, Your affectionate Son,

"STUART."

Mr. Moxhay read the letter slowly, and gave it to Margaret, who had brought it up from the hall, and was waiting for orders at the bedside.

"Read this."

As she read, her fingers grew cold and trembled.

"Did you know this?"

She snatched for the slate.

"I KNEW JOHN HAD LEFT SCHOOL. I DIDN'T KNOW ALL STUART SAYS AND THINK HE——"

"Give it. Quickly."

He read what she had written, and shouted, "What do you think? What does it matter what you think?"

"PLEASE, DEAR FATHER, TRY TO BE CALM, OR——"

He took the slate from her again.

"Wire to Haybrook at once. Tell Hector to come here and bring his boy—immediately. I give him six hours to be here. Get off and send that telegram. Get off, I say."

"PLEASE, FATHER, I CAN'T LEAVE YOU LIKE THIS."

He was not displeased by her solicitude.

"Do as I say. You can ring for Watts."

She rang the bell, and on her way downstairs met Watts, the male attendant.

"Will you please go to Mr. Moxhay at once?" she said. "I'm afraid he's been agitated by a letter which came this morning. If he asks about it, say that I'm doing what he told me to do, and that Mr. Hector should be here soon after luncheon."

She was still carrying Stuart's letter, she found. Perhaps it was as well, or her father would show it to Watts, from whom few secrets were hid.

She wrote her telegram at the desk in the drawing-room.

"Hector Moxhay, Haybrook, Ramshott. Please bring John to see father as soon as possible. Most urgent. Margaret."

Anyone, she reflected, might open the telegram. Hector might be hunting that morning. No, not so soon after Maggie's death. Does one hunt soon after deaths? But he might be out. She rang for a maid and gave her the telegram to take to the post office. Hardly had she done so, when she heard Watts' heavy footsteps on the stairs.

"If you please, Miss, will you bring up the letter the master gave you?"

As she went into Mr. Moxhay's bedroom, she saw Euphemia, perplexed no doubt by all the running up and down stairs, peering over the banisters from the landing above.

Euphemia went back to her room at the end of the passage, and sat down opposite the window. It was cold, but the March sun shone brightly into the open windows of the opposite house. The man in the room under the roof was having breakfast in front of a big fire. Euphemia could see his back and the end of the parting in his fair hair. He was wearing his usual brown-and-green silk dressing-gown. She could not see what he was eating. "That arm-chair by the screen," she thought, "will need covering again soon. He ought to have the cretonne with chrysanthemums that's on the sofa." It was a charming picture, intimate, cheerful, comfortable. What was he reading in the paper? What was he thinking of? What were his plans for the day? For him what adventures, what successes, were in store?

The answering telegram was brought to Margaret at half-past twelve.

"Moxhay, 12 Adelaide Square, London. Hector left for Cannes yesterday taking John to Paris, where friends. Rosa."

V

APRIL

Mr. Moxhay's first letter to Hector contained warnings, threats and violent advice. Margaret did not see it, though she saw Hector's reply, calm, almost affectionate, but not submissive, two days after it arrived. Mr. Moxhay wrote again, and after sending the letter, became so ill that Dr. Miard called in Dr. Frost. There was, said Dr. Frost, no cause for great alarm. The sea breeze at Shoreston would work wonders. Meanwhile, the emotions must not be taxed. He was even bold enough to suggest to Mr. Moxhay that, in the interests of his health, he should reconcile himself with Hector.

Margaret had written Hector a letter full of qualified understatements, and many times made desperate plans for visiting him. She had enough money for the journey. But clearly, it was impossible. She was needed at home more than ever. What right had she to interfere? Perhaps Hector wished for a breach. Why should he cling any longer to the clan? "Then," she thought, "he will come no more to Adelaide Square. No more Christmasses for him. And how shall I ever see him? Perella will hardly dare to see him either, as long as she wishes to be one of us. And she will wish it, for some time."

They were miserable days, and she spied on every post. Stuart called at the house from time to time, and she found it hard to speak to him. Archibald was unwell, and Cyril Clark deputised for him. Finally, Mr. Moxhay sent a grumbling offer of peace, and Margaret went to Shoreston to see the house-agent.

They had been to Shoreston for eleven summers, and Margaret could no longer distinguish them clearly. There had been the summer during the war when a submarine had been seen in the

43

bay; the summer when the chimney of Seamew was struck by lightning and 'Genia fainted; the summer when Mortimer and Perella were love-making; the summer when she had acted in "A Winter's Tale"—in aid of something. She did not know whether she had been happier at Shoreston than in London, and tried to think the question irrelevant. At the beginning of each of the last three visits, she could not help wondering how many more visits there were to be.

The fact that Seamew was not to be let before Whitsun seemed to make a great change. She saw the ugly house, in the middle of Marine Parade, the "Guinevere Royal Pension" on one side and "Westward Ho" on the other, as she walked from the station to the house-agent's. The woodwork was being painted a bright green, and a stand for flowers in pots had been fixed above the porch. "It would look nice to see ivy geraniums trailing over the porch," Phoebe had said wistfully, "but I suppose as you only take the place for the summer, it's hardly worth the expense." Perella had been listening and smiled. Margaret felt suddenly sorry that they were not going to Seamew. Euphemia had enjoyed sitting in the bay window of the drawing-room, and watching the guests of the "Guinevere Royal Pension" having coffee on their little verandah, after dinner. The guests there dressed, as a rule, unlike those at Westward Ho. Other people, when one watches them, usually look happy.

The house-agent motored her to Cliff House. It was over two miles from the town and stood on a small headland by itself. Margaret had passed it once or twice when taking a walk. It was a square stone house, and looked dismal after the bright array on the promenade. The garden was wind-swept and neglected, and apart from narrow borders round the house, and a few crescent-shaped flower-beds in which grew some stunted euonymus, was formed by an expanse of coarse, unmown lawn, which sloped steeply down to a four-foot stone wall built round the edge of the cliff. A doorway in the wall gave access to a little platform of rock, from which a series of roughly cut foot-holes zigzagged down to the shingle. Projecting ledges of rock made the place unsuitable for murder or suicide.

An old lady showed Margaret round the house. The morning-room—the drawing-room—the conservatory. In front of the dining-room the ground sloped so steeply that if one stood a little way from the French window, one had the illusion of being in the saloon of a ship with the sea immediately outside. Margaret watched the placid grey sea with enjoyment, and hardly heard the old lady's conversation.

"After a death, you know, one is glad to get away. . . . My husband. . . . Married forty-seven years next June. . . . But I am afraid you may find it rather quiet. . . . Quite in the country here. . . . I wonder how you will amuse yourself. . . . Bathing. . . . A large family, did you say?"

"Yes, very large. At least, my father is an invalid, and has an attendant, and sometimes a nurse. My younger sister lives at home, and I have brothers who visit us with their wives. And there are their children."

The first floor—the best bedroom—the dressing-room—the visitors' room. Another bedroom—another.

"On this side, of course, you get the morning sun. And almost everywhere you get the sea. Look, here it is again. You see how the bay bends round. A little peninsular it is, indeed."

The second floor.

"The maids sleep here, but there are still three very good rooms upstairs, if you need those. On this side, of course, you get the morning sun. . . . Now, would you care to see the garden? I'm afraid, outside the conservatory, we never trouble about flowers. But, coming from London, you won't miss them. They do so badly by the sea. Nothing grows, except the grass and those coarse shrubs. But it's nice to have it all so natural, isn't it? First, though, you should see the kitchens. This way. Is it you who do the house-keeping?"

"Yes."

"My youngest daughter wouldn't stay at home. Girls are so restless nowadays."

Butler's pantry—servants' hall—kitchen—scullery—larder.

Margaret asked a practical question.

"I suppose, even in summer, it's cool and airy?"

"Indeed, yes. We get our milk from—but of course you know the Shoreston shops. Strangers sometimes like to be told where to go. We can go this way into the garden. Three little steps, mind. . . . Everything leads to the sea. How calm it is to-day. Sometimes, the waves. . . ."

"And now," said the agent, who had been following them, hat in hand, "a few little matters of business."

In her dreams that night, Margaret was walking in the gardens on the Shoreston cliffs. It was an evening of prolonged and many-coloured twilight. Bright little clouds passed quickly across the sky. The air was full of sudden scents from the flowers in the gardens, and sudden strains of music borne by a gusty breeze from an invisible band.

As Margaret walked, shapes and shadows darted across the path and lost themselves in darkness. The path was full of people, the crowd coming back from evening service at St. Jude's, sailors, and soldiers, and other more mysterious persons who wore masks and sidled stealthily along the laurel hedges. Everything moved, and Margaret herself hurried onwards with a feeling of alarm; for someone had tampered with the paths, and now and again she saw just in front of her a dark hole, which she knew was very deep. The people who pursued her were not those who brushed against her, but she dared not look back to see how far they were behind. Yet there was no chance of their not recognising her, as they were her relations.

At last, she saw the steps leading to the sea—a long marble flight roofed in with a plaster ceiling. As she turned to go down, a hand struck her on the back of the head. Dizzily she ran down, with the sound of feet pattering behind. As she went, the steps grew bigger and she had to jump from each one to the next, till finally she jumped too far forward and fell outwards through the slanting passage, which she now saw was shut in at the bottom with two massive gold doors. As she struck them, they opened.

The palace stood amongst tall chestnut trees. The lawns which led to the majestic entrance glittered with morning dew, while horse-chestnuts, half out of their cases, lay about the grass, silky and brown in the bright sunshine. "This palace," she said, "is for my honour and glory." And as she spoke, she raised her arms as if they were wings, and springing over a tall fountain that played in the middle of the courtyard, alighted on a broad balcony whence she could see the vastness of her territories.

Her relations, shabby little men wearing bowler hats, and untidy women with string bags, sat like trippers on the grass by the door, and ate out of paper bags. As she watched them with uneasiness, one of them, a man whom she could not identify, stood up and said, "What have you to give us?"

She did not answer, and distressed at being tongue-tied she leant back against the wall hoping that her grey dress would be indistinguishable from the stone.

"What have you to give us?"

Mechanically she pointed to the park and said, "Make yourselves free of it."

"That is not enough. You know what we have come for."

The voice ceased to be that of the poor relation, and seemed to come from inside herself. Indeed, it was she, in a sense, who spoke the whole of the duologue which followed.

"Take everything."

"How can we take what you don't give? Why do you shrink away? Why are you so stiff and severe? Are you afraid of laughing or crying? Why are you colder and harder than other people?"

"You ask that because you don't know me. My heart is not on my sleeve. I feel all that you feel and more."

"Show us what you feel."

"It would hurt me too much. But I share all your troubles."

"Then you are afraid to help us?"

"No, not if I must."

"Do you not see you must?"

"Yes—but give me a little time."

"You have lived thirty-six years. Aren't you strong enough yet?"

"I am stronger than any of you."

"Then give your strength."

"Take it."

"Do you still pity yourself?"

"Not now. If I did, I could not help you."

"How much can you bear?"

"Everything. Take my strength, take my life and use it as you wish. Put your whole trust in me, and I will save you."

"And your love?"

"Take that too."

VI

MAY

THEY had been settled about a fortnight at Cliff House when Alec Kithen called. Mr. Moxhay was in bed, but the others were quite a large party—Jenny Clark, her husband and baby, and Phoebe, all four of them staying in the house, besides Margaret and Euphemia, and Perella who was in rooms at Shoreston with her baby. They liked Alec, and were impressed when Perella made him talk about himself and his step-brother. No Moxhay had ever headed a procession of ten taxis which drove at breakneck speed round Piccadilly Circus till the police interfered. "I suppose Kitty's photo was in the *Mirror* again the next day," Perella asked. It was. "And not to be outdone, you took a new studio on the strength of it?" "Probably." "I used to love your Bohemianism. Do you remember that naughty little song of yours,

> *On l'a vue*
> *Toute nue?*

How did it go?"

He laughed. Was it embarrassment or modesty?

As he was about to drive Perella back to Shoreston, she said, so that Margaret could hear: "And mind, when I leave Shoreston, you'll come and see Margaret, won't you? Write to him, Margaret, if he doesn't. He's shy. So long."

Margaret did not suppose she would ever see him again.

"Did you like him, Auntie Margaret?" Phoebe asked.

"Yes, very much."

"He's very good-looking."

"A pretty little dancing-bear."

"Oh, Auntie Margaret! Did you like him, Auntie Euphemia?"

"Not specially."

49

"Didn't you think him good-looking, Jenny?"

"Yes, very."

"Now, dear," said her husband.

Then, as it was still raining they went into the dining-room and wrote down all the geographical terms they could think of beginning with G. If Mr. Moxhay had allowed them to play cards in the house, it would have been easier to keep them amused in wet weather.

Ten days later Alec called again. Perella and the Clarks had gone back to London, though Phoebe was still staying on. Mr. Moxhay was downstairs, and the visitor was introduced on the slate. The moment the conversation became lively, Mr. Moxhay asked what they were talking about, and Margaret was glad when Alec said good-bye.

"It was good of you to come," she said.

"Not at all. May I come again?"

"Do, if it amuses you. Are you staying in the country all the summer?"

"As far as I can see. I've nowhere to go to in London."

"What about your studio?"

"I've given it up. I can't afford one at present."

"But your painting?"

"I never painted. I wrote a bit. Things seem to be drying up now."

"What do you do?"

"I drive about in my little car—on my mother's petrol."

He waved and went.

"If he comes again," Margaret thought, "I shall wonder why he comes. Is it Phoebe? Or Euphemia? Or does he think we're richer than we are, and will finance plays and newspapers for him?"

She met him the third time a week later, while she was shopping in Shoreston.

"I was going to call on you this afternoon."

"Then I wish I hadn't to tell you that my niece has left, my sister's in bed with a cold, and my father's also in bed."

"I hope it's nothing serious."

"The doctor doesn't think so."

"Then may I come to tea?"

"I wish you would. But if you do, come very early, as I shall have to sit with my father after five."

He came early and catechised her. It was impossible to escape from his questions. She had not thought that there was so much force in him.

What did she do? The housekeeping. And in London? The housekeeping. What did she read? Arnold Bennett, H. G. Wells, Hugh Walpole, Somerset Maugham, the *Morning Post*, *Punch* and *Good Housekeeping*. Did she go to the theatre? Oh yes. Often? Not very. How many times that year? Only once, when she had taken some nieces to a pantomime. How many times the year before? Four or five. The year before that? Rather oftener. Concerts? Sometimes. Did she play the piano? Yes, a little. What? Haydn, Mozart, Bach's easier Preludes and Inventions, Handel, Beethoven's earlier Sonatas, and studies of all kinds, Heller, Cramer, Jensen. She did not play well enough to please other people, or music which other people cared for. Art? She had been to the Academy the year before. That year she supposed she would miss it. Was she interested in china, glass, carpets, furniture and house decoration? Not really, and if she had such interests, there would be little scope for them. Was she well-informed? Did she go to museums and lectures? Very seldom. Religion and philanthropy? Did she do church work? Very little. Slumming? She had tried three times but the women in charge had made difficulties. In the end her father had forbidden her to go, in case she brought back an infectious disease. Did she get on well with her family? Oh yes, very well.

"And now," she said, "it's my turn to ask you about yourself."

But at that moment Watts came in to say that the master wished her to sit with him.

That evening, she wondered again why Alec had come to tea. This time he had known that he would find her alone. But knowing that, perhaps he thought it would have been rude not to come.

And why those almost impertinent questions? Perhaps because they were the easiest form of conversation. Or did he find her a "human document"? Was she material for a character in a new play or novel? Or was it really that he thought the Moxhays richer than they were, and hoped to have plays and reviews financed by them? The alliance of brains and birth with industry? No doubt Perella had exaggerated ideas of her father-in-law's wealth, and had passed them on.

Four days later Alec telephoned and asked if she would let him take her for a drive and to tea in Shoreston. She said that she must first see if her father needed her that afternoon. Mr. Moxhay was suspicious when he was shown her request on the slate, but gave a grudging consent. Alec came round with his motor at half past three.

"The country here is particularly uninteresting," he said. "Don't you think so?"

"Yes, but there's the sea, which is nearly always interesting."

"Provided you're not on it."

"Yes."

After a pause he said, "I suppose someone you were very fond of was killed in the war."

"Yes."

"I was afraid so."

"But," she added, making an admission not only to him, but to herself, "it wasn't really so important as I tried to think. There have been other more important things in my life."

"Do you mean—of the same kind?"

"Oh, no, quite different."

"Could you tell me them?"

"No, I'm afraid not."

In Shoreston he took her to a building on the front, which was new that year. It was an annexe to the best hotel. An electric sign outside gave it the name of the Royal Banana.

It was a Saturday and the place was nearly full. The middle of the room was given up to a swarm of dancers. Alec could only find a table near the band. The noise made conversation impossible, and instead of talking Margaret found herself watching the blond saxophonist, who kept playing a phrase of four ascending crotchets followed by two descending triplets of quavers and a minim. With each of the crotchets he took a bold pace forward. With the triplets he scampered backwards. There was in his antics something clever, fascinating and obscene. It would be a change, she thought, if he could replace the Christmas hymn-singing in Adelaide Square.

The tea was expensive, but not otherwise remarkable.

They drove back slowly by a devious route.

"Are you wondering," Alec asked, "why I took you there?"

"Naturally."

"I wondered what effect it would have on you."

"Well?"

"I can't gather, yet. Will you please express yourself?"

"I liked the saxophone."

"Have you ever wanted to go to Cannes, or Deauville or Biarritz?"

"My sister and I once spent a fortnight in a pension at Étretat."

"Superb."

"Are you laughing at me, or am I a 'human document'?"

"Inhuman."

"I didn't," he went on, "take you to the Royal Banana to dazzle you with its *faux luxe*."

"But to see what effect it would have on me?"

No one, as far as she could remember, had ever taken her to anything to see what effect it would have upon her. Such experiments in psychology were not in the Moxhay tradition.

"It had," he said, "presumably no effect. Would you like, do you think, to get up at midday and amuse yourself for two hours in front of a dressing-table covered with five-guinea bottles of scent, come down about two to an exquisite luncheon, if you hadn't ordered it to be served in your room, and then spend the afternoon lying on an expensive beach or going to the races or watching your admirers play polo?"

"Go on."

"Tea about six—marvellous little savoury sandwiches that you don't get in England. Cocktails. A rest. More dressing-table. Dinner at ten. Then the casino for a few hours, and a night club to finish up with, where you would grow slightly abandoned after a dozen glasses of champagne and allow your principal admirer to snap a pearl necklace round your neck. What effect would that have on you?"

"I can't think. I should do it all so badly. Why not suggest something else for me—that I should become principal of an enormous chicken farm, superintending acres of hen-houses and millions of eggs?"

"Because it's too like you. Are you an efficient housekeeper?"

"I do my best. I come from a business family."

"What business?"

"We make textile machinery, or rather we used to make it. My father still doesn't take artificial silk seriously, and so——"

"What?"

"I oughtn't to tell you these secrets, especially as they're so dull."

"I'm not a trade rival."

"The depression in the Bradford wool trade has been rather a blow for us. We're by no means as well off as perhaps some people imagine."

He looked at her not without consternation.

"You don't mean anything disastrous is likely to happen to you all?"

"Not in the least. My father has more than we need to live on, in government securities. But the 'slump', as they call it, is disheartening for my brother."

"Which one is that? I thought you had several brothers."

"Only three now—and of them only one is in the business. You met his son-in-law, Cyril Clark, the first time you called on us."

"Oh, did I. Tell me, why do you suppose Perella brought us together?"

"I suppose because she thought we should enjoy making one another's acquaintance."

When he left her at Cliff House, it was a little late. Mr. Moxhay was in a bad mood.

"Where have you been?"

"Motoring with Mr. Kithen. You said I could. Don't you remember?"

"Has he proposed to you?"

"No."

"Is there any chance that he will?"

"I don't know."

"Are you a fool, girl? Don't stand there blushing like that. I asked you if there was a chance."

"I suppose there is a chance, though——"

"That'll do. Then understand this, please. I'm not going to have you throwing yourself away on a penniless nincompoop who wants your money. If you marry the fellow, you get nothing from me. Your place is here, at home. Your sister needs you, and so do I. Do you understand?"

"I've had no thoughts of marrying him."

"That's a lie. Send Watts to me."

With cheeks still burning, she wiped the unlovely sentences away.

Euphemia was lying on her bed. She looked feverish and restless. The roulette wheel, some papers and a novel made an untidy heap on the floor.

"Are you sure you oughtn't to see the doctor?" Margaret asked, after a few preliminary words.

"Quite sure. I'm not ill."

"I wish you'd let me take your temperature."

"All right, if it'll give you any peace. The thermometer's in there."

She pointed to a corner cupboard. Margaret fetched the thermometer, gave it to her sister and picking up the novel, pretended to read it, though she kept one eye on her sister to be sure that the temperature was properly taken.

"Normal."

"Let me see. Yes, it is. I wonder why you seem so hot. It's quite cool outside. Is anything troubling you?"

Euphemia scowled.

"I hate this place. Why are we wasting time here? The whole summer, wasted—spent looking at the sea. Look at it now—look out of the window. Flat, dull, empty. You might as well stare at a finger-bowl. I hate it. I want to go back to London."

Margaret sighed.

"To Adelaide Square?"

"Yes."

"Oh, not yet. What is there in London? What is there to look at there? Especially from your window, which looks on to nothing but the wall of a house and roofs. Don't you prefer the sea to that?"

"No, I don't. I like my room in London. You're always trying to interfere with it. Why can't you leave me alone?"

"Why won't you let me help you?"

"You can't help."

The roulette wheel caught Margaret's attention.

"Do you still play your game with that?" she asked. "I wish you'd let me into the secret."

"I only keep a record of the numbers as they turn up. I've told you that already."

"How often has 10 turned up?"

Euphemia stretched languidly for a sheet of paper.

"Five thousand eight hundred and four times. It's quite a good number," she added grudgingly.

"And 19?"

"Six thousand three hundred and seventy-five times. It's top."

"What does it mean?"

Euphemia looked at her with the cunning of an animal.

"Why, that the wheel works wrongly, of course."

"And 11?"

"Five thousand seven hundred and twenty times. It's done much better lately."

There was a note of triumph and quiet pride in her voice.

"Why do you want 11 to win, Phemy? What does it mean?"

"It means I shall—no, I won't tell you. It would take too long. Besides, I'm not altogether sure."

VII

JUNE

"Lole, Lopside, Loda, Lultanas, Lime-juice, Liphons (3) do. Lole."
The book-keeper at the big store in Shoreston made capital S
and T like L.

Margaret was doing the housekeeping books in her bedroom
that faced the sea. It was the last day in June. The sea hardly moved,
and a vast semicircle of mountainous clouds, their regular bases
ten degrees above the horizon, made Cliff House the centre of a
universe. The clouds were slowly gliding inwards, and seemed to
compress the air till it was more solid than the sea. Suddenly the
air and the whole house quivered at five deep explosions—blasting at Midhampton quarry eight miles away. Margaret looked at
her watch. It was half past three. Blasting was only allowed at that
time and at half past eleven. The ledger in which she was making
an analysis of the books had to be ready for Mr. Moxhay by a quarter past five. Till then, he would be sleeping. There was plenty
of time. She had managed her catering badly during the previous
week. Every item came to more than the average. (She had had
to work out the averages and memorise them). Over the essen-
tials of life Mr. Moxhay was not mean. He was prepared to pay
for as much milk, meat and bread as his family would eat, but he
made careful inquiries about luxuries, cherries, tins of sardines and
chocolate biscuits.

"Lole."

How was it they had had "lole" three times? She looked idly
at the horizon, while searching for an explanation. A broad semi-
circular shadow ran round the edge of the sea, leaving a thin strip
of clear water beyond. Nearer at hand were other shadows, less
regular and more complex. As one watched them, they seemed to
rise out of the flat surface, forming dark hills over which passed a

gentle and transparent movement, as if a delicate vegetation were putting forth a quick bloom. Then the hills themselves, overladen, dissolved and sank, and distant gulls, like scraps of white paper whirling in a sunlit street, flashed upwards out of nothing, catching and losing the light. The sea was as she enjoyed it most—full of quiet and concealed interests, like the lives of people of whom one does not read in the newspapers.

"Lole."

On Saturday night the curate at the Parish Church had come to dinner. On Tuesday——

There was a sound of panting and a heavy tread on the stairs. Margaret's eyes left the sea and narrowed into a firm alertness. But when Alice came in, she did not say, "Please Miss, the master would like you to go to his room," but, "Please, Miss, Mr. Hector has called."

"Mr. Hector?"

"Yes, Miss. He's in the garden."

"All right, Alice. I'll be down in five minutes."

In five minutes she had finished the books.

"Hector!"

"So this is the nest. Do you like it?"

"Immensely. Let's go and sit lower down. There's a seat at the top of the rock. Unless you want——"

"No, I don't."

"Euphemia's resting, and father's asleep. Have you come from London?"

"Yes, in my new car. A two-seater."

"Hector!"

"You forget, I'm rich."

"Here we are. Do you like our view?"

"No. It reminds me of all the pale women who are staring at it for hundreds of miles either side of us."

"Thank you for thinking of me."

"You're less pale."

"Have you been in London long?"

"For five days."

"And did you call at Archibald's?"

"No, I'm afraid not. I'll go when I get back."

Archibald was still not well, and Margaret understood and excused the form of cowardice which had kept Hector from visiting him.

"I saw none of the family," he went on, "except Winifred's back in a tube station. I avoided her."

"How is Rosa?"

"They're all well. She and Rosamund went to her father's a few days ago. John's at Ramshott, staying with Kenrick, his music master."

"Have you got John a tutor yet?"

"No. I really don't see why I should. He's got this musical bee in his bonnet, and as he can read and write and do simple arithmetic, I don't see why he should bother with Greek or algebra."

"But what about going to Oxford?"

"He doesn't want to go."

They were silent for a little. The moment Margaret's thoughts were taken from the sea, they found material to trouble them. Why had he come, she wondered. What did he wish to say to her?

When he began to talk again, it was in an elaborate and devious strain that was unusual with him. She could barely remember any real "conversation" with him. Her memory presented him in glimpses, smiling and saying, "By Jove, what a fine melon", or "Let me open that tin for you", smiling and going away with a wave of the hand—never settling down to a talk and fighting towards an object in it.

This time, his conversation seemed to have an object. He spoke of loneliness, carelessly at first, then more gravely. Why is it that one doesn't enjoy going to the theatre alone? Eating alone? Drinking alone? It was not that one wished to talk the whole time, of course. And then, dying. (The transition was abrupt.) The awfulness of death must lie chiefly in its essential loneliness, part of oneself going out pitifully to those in tears round the bed, and another part drifting onwards in solitary horror. Suicide pacts? At the last minute they were always broken. Dying in crowds, arms linked? That was better, perhaps—if you could be sure that the pressure of your neighbour's arm would weaken as yours weakened—that in the supreme moment, the voice of a companion would say, "I feel this too".

And when one is alive, it is when one feels oneself most strongly that one feels most alone. One comes home after an outing, laughter and noisy voices still echoing in the ears, and says, "Now, what of it all? Am I any less alone for having been with all those people?"

Of course, there are forms of self-forgetfulness, narcotics, absorption in the herd. But what one wants is not self-forgetfulness, but an increased self-consciousness enhanced with the knowledge that others are also conscious of oneself. "To have," said Margaret, "a lover, who would say, 'when you die, I die.'"

"Lovers," he answered, "are unfaithful. I mean a union of two wills, so close as to seem in the same body. Why aren't we born in pairs—Siamese twins, if you like—two minds sharing one nervous system?"

It was indeed unlike him, to talk in such a strain.

"Have you an ideal," she said nervously, "with whom you could live for ever? I always thought you were one to uproot yourself—to cut ties—not to cling to your old friends—I mean, as Archibald keeps going back to his old school."

"I don't ask to live for others," he said, "I ask others to live for me."

"You would find that very tedious."

"Of course. But I didn't know we were discussing things from a practical point of view."

His anger at her commonplace reply grieved her.

"I read this morning," she said, knowing that she was contributing little to the conversation, "that we all attach too much importance to our personal emotions. Our private fears and wishes, the article said, and even love, are of no account when compared with the general development of society. It used the phrase 'the deplorable luxury of an over-developed individualism'."

"Rubbish!"

"Why?"

"There are so many answers. In the first place, it is an imperti-
nence of the writer to say that my private feelings are of no account
compared to the general development of society. They may be of
much greater account to me. These people will use phrases like
'are of account', 'are valuable', and 'matter', without considering
to whom something is of account, or valuable, or matters. Nothing can 'matter' in the abstract. It has to 'matter' to some definite
person, or group of people. And even then you don't get a standard by simply counting heads. A dog race may matter to ten thousand people, and a piece of poetry to five people. It doesn't follow
that the dog race matters more than the poetry. It's like saying that
a ton is always better than an ounce, measuring by quantity and
ignoring quality. And you can't add up feelings like happiness or
grief, either, and say the happiness of three people makes three
happinesses and is therefore more important than mine which is
only one happiness—but this is boring you."

A little conscious of having rambled on too far, he dislodged a
splinter of rock and flung it down at the sea.

"All the same," said Margaret, "I think I am happiest when I
don't think about it."

"An admirable and practical maxim," he said ironically. "But
your writer was laying down the theory of the thing. In theory,
wouldn't it be pleasanter to be happy and think about it at the
same time? Besides, you're speaking for yourself. You're——"

"Say it."

"No."

During the silence which followed, she felt that he was trying to
banish his unusual mood, and to become as he generally appeared
to her. She had to be quick, if she was to use the opportunity he
had given her.

"Marriage," she said, "is supposed to be a cure for all that sort
of thing."

"What sort of thing?"

"Isolation—the feeling of loneliness."

He looked at her with admiration for her insight.

"It may be—sometimes. Margaret, this is a secret. I shan't be living with Rosa any more. She's divorcing me."

She waited for him to continue.

"You know why, don't you?" he asked. "I mean, you knew we didn't care for one another? Why should we bother to go on?"

"The children."

"She takes Rosamund. I take John."

"Rosamund will miss you."

"Not very much. She has a terribly bright nature. At any rate, her possible grief doesn't make me feel bound to spoil all the rest of my life. This is not to be mentioned, yet."

He climbed stiffly to his feet.

"You'll come and see father?" she asked.

"How is he?"

"Very much the same—better, if anything."

"I really don't think I will."

"If you don't, he'll be—hurt."

"Must he know I've called?"

"Alice will tell Watts, and Watts will tell him."

"It can't be helped. I haven't time."

"Oh, Hector."

"If he sleeps till five—and, of course, I couldn't disturb him— really Margaret, I don't see why, because he's permanently thirty-three years older than I am, I should live in permanent obedience to his unexpressed wishes. I don't expect that kind of thing from John —and over John I've got a very direct financial hold."

"Of course, Hector, if you want to break away from the family——"

"I'm not breaking away. I shall be down here again soon. Sunday afternoon, perhaps. What a painful peacemaker you are, Margaret. Are you afraid of him cutting me out of his will? He's done that long ago. Besides, even if he hasn't—one can wait too long for some things. Come and look at my car. It's a very cheap one, really."

Turning their backs to the sea, they walked up the sloping

garden and round to the front of the house. Hector's motor stood in shadow by the porch. Margaret admired it. An early edition of the evening paper was lying on the seat.

"Would you like this?" he asked.

"Thanks."

"I saw a poster saying 'Peer killed in accident', and had to buy it in case it was Rosa's father. It wasn't, of course. Good-bye, my dear."

"Good-bye, Hector. And you must go to Archibald's. Their letters are so vague and contradictory. Do write to us and say how he really is."

"Doesn't Stuart write?"

"He does, but I never know how far I can believe him."

"Stuart is usually misguided, but always honest."

She looked doubtful.

"He is," he continued, "honest over everything, except that he's really lost his faith. That's what makes him such a stage clergyman. I suspect he lost it the moment he was ordained. Till then it bubbled up inside him. Now he hasn't any natural impulse to be what he is, and so plays this burlesque part in order to deceive himself. He wouldn't try to deceive us. His character is really most admirable. We're not on speaking terms."

"Is this sarcasm?"

"No, not at all."

He gave her the paper, started the engine, waved, and drove neatly through the narrow gate.

Margaret met Euphemia in the hall.

"Hector's been, Phemy."

"Oh."

"If father asks about it, we must say——" And she explained how the breach of courtesy could best be smoothed over.

"All right. Is that the paper?"

"Yes. Here it is."

As Margaret went upstairs, she heard Euphemia calling.

"Margaret, Lord Kithen's been killed."

"*Lord* Kithen?"

"At half-past ten this morning, it says, Lord Kithen was knocked down by a motor bus in Piccadilly. That's a good death."

Margaret was more horrified by Euphemia's comment than startled by the news.

"How do you mean," she would have liked to ask, "a good death? Why are you classifying deaths?"

But she dared say nothing, and went to her room, where she collected the account books. Then she went to the landing below, and knocked at her father's door. Watts opened it, and her father, seeing the door move, shouted a gruff "Come in".

"Lole."

VIII

JULY

NEXT morning they all, including Mr. Moxhay, read the *Morning Post's* account of Lord Kithen's death. He had been killed while saving an old woman from the traffic—a fine end to an inglorious career.

Throughout the morning Mr. Moxhay was gentle and docile. When he mentioned Hector's visit, reported to him by Watts, he simply said he was sorry he had been sleeping at the time. Margaret was alarmed at the absence of a reproach. In the afternoon, he got up and told them to bring his chair down to the terrace in front of the sea. Margaret and Euphemia sat, one on either side of him. After a few minutes, he sent Euphemia away on an errand.

Suddenly he said, "I'm proud of my children. I thank God for it."

"You've been good daughters," he continued, while Margaret was wondering how to reply, "and I'm not ungrateful. Of course, I don't want to lose you, but if a time comes when I must, I shall bear it as best I may."

"WHY SHOULD YOU LOSE US?" the pencil squeaked.

"Well," he said, "Nature must have her way. Youth calls to youth. Won't you play something, Margaret? Though I can't hear, I like to watch your fingers."

It was a startling request. The last time Margaret had played the piano in his presence—a foggy November evening, in Adelaide Square—he had accused her of being unfeeling.

She went into the drawing-room and sat down on the piano stool. Her father could see her through the bay window. For his benefit she played a piece full of scale passages, and rocked her wrists and elbows in a way which her teacher would not have admired. To the notes themselves she paid no heed. She was grieved at what

66

she knew her father's thoughts to be, and ashamed that he did not take more pains to conceal them. Why was it, she wondered, conscious of the ugliness of her movements and the degradation that was being forced upon her, why was it that every event which befell the Moxhays became at once flattened and vulgarised? Why had they, as a family, no power of giving their actions a pictorial aloofness? She had been reading earlier in the day a biography which introduced several eighteenth-century characters, and the contrast between the manner in which these persons pursued their ends, selfish, vicious and ignoble though they often were, and the manner in which the Moxhays built up the landmarks in their lives, struck her with painful vividness. History, no doubt, records the making of innumerable dynastic marriages, based on every odious motive. But, she thought, one pictures them, these marriage-makers, brides and grooms, going about their business against a tapestried background, pacing through vast and panelled rooms, opening, with hurried but not ungraceful hands, the secret drawer in the old walnut secretaire, in search for documents sealed with red wax, turning sharply at a footfall behind the massive curtains, drawing swords, pouring poison from crystal phials into goblets of brown wine, and receiving triumphs and disasters when they came, with a solemn inclination of the head, a smile, a gesture of the fan. How surely they would move, with a dignity and purpose which made no crime unpardonable, no trickery contemptible. Well might their descendants say with a careless pride, "The will, of course, was forged by my great-great-grandmother, the king's mistress. . . ."

"Youth calls to youth. Won't you play something, Margaret?"

"How different. And yet . . ." Still playing fervently, she rebuked herself for the uncharitable thoughts, which sinned against her difficult ideal, the pride which roused ambitions, the resentment at the insult to her pride.

On the terrace, Mr. Moxhay was asleep.

Throughout the rest of the month, Margaret would wonder, when she sat alone, how soon her father would repeat his suggestions. A form of delicacy or caution prevented him from speaking outright, but he made his wish continually apparent. A new Debrett lay amongst the books beside his bed. He would read aloud the accounts of fashionable weddings in the newspapers. He ordered all letters to be brought to him as soon as they arrived, hoping in vain for the sight of the Kithen crest on an envelope. Alec, indeed, wrote to Margaret twice, but on plain paper. She wondered why he wrote. There was nothing in his letters to tell her. Often she asked herself if her family was rich enough to make her eligible. Had he been still a "younger son", he might have fallen for her, but now, surrounded as he must be by more brilliant competitors than she. . . . It was not unpleasant to think, "if he asks me to marry him, it will be because he loves me", and it was a relief, too, to consider the match only from Alec's point of view. Her own feelings she could not analyse. He was a refuge, a way of escape, which on no account she ought to take, though she could give no reason for this conviction.

But this suspense, her father's eagerness, and a hidden war between two parts of her own nature were of small account compared with her anxiety over Euphemia, who kept more and more to her room, and grew daily more irritable, more difficult to approach, and in body, despite the sea and the fresh air, frailer and paler. Margaret watched her with a fearful secrecy, asked careful questions and pondered long and miserably over ambiguous replies. And whatever trouble, mental or physical, she imagined she had detected, she took the entire blame upon herself. Twice she confronted her sister with the doctor, but Euphemia was so unresponsive and so openly contemptuous of her visitor, that no good came of the meetings. Twice also, she spoke to her father, but he, resentful of all illness save his own, brushed her fears aside and told her to mind her own business.

She wrote to Hector, who replied, "These troubles are only of your own making. I know what you feel about Euphemia—the absurd complex that bothers you, and makes you see illness where there is none. Forget the whole business and think of the wretchedness of your own existence. Be discontented. Remind yourself twenty times a day, how you, an intelligent and attractive woman of thirty-six, are squandering your life in an uncomfortable house, full of selfish half-wits and overpaid servants, deprived of friends, all reasonable interests, and even reasonable affection. Make plans for your own future, and be hard."

For two or three days the letter brought her comfort.

IX

AUGUST

A

One beautiful day, soon after August Bank Holiday, Margaret was climbing up the steps in the rock after a bathe, when Euphemia came running to meet her and shouted, "I'm going to London. I'm going to London to-day."

Margaret was astonished.

"You?" she said, "But why?"

For a moment Euphemia seemed to have forgotten the reason. Then she answered quickly, "Because it's time someone went to see Archibald and find out how ill he really is. Father's not satisfied with 'Genia's letters, and wants me to ask her some questions."

"You?"

"Why not?"

"Of course, there's no reason why—but, a lovely day like this—he can't have meant to send you——"

"I want to go."

Her face was full of a doll-like obstinacy.

"But, Phemy, it's absurd."

"I'm catching the train at 2.32."

"I must see father."

"Margaret, don't you interfere!"

"No, Phemy. But I can't think he wants you to go."

"Don't you believe me, then? Why is it that you so often seem to treat me differently from other people? Do you think I can't take care of myself?"

"Of course you can. But it seems such a shame for you to be sent off, a day like to-day."

"We've had so many days like to-day. I want to go."

The air and the garden quivered with a deep explosion. Half past-eleven.

"It may be awkward for 'Genia to put you up, Phemy. And you wouldn't want to go to Stuart's."

"What about Adelaide Square?"

"But you can't go there. It's all shut up, except for the Joneses. You'd find nothing but dust-sheets about. They couldn't manage dinner, or anything."

"I've made all arrangements."

"Well——"

"Why this mountain out of a mole-hill?" Margaret thought, turning for a moment to look at the sea. Then with an effort of will she went to her father's room.

He was not harsh, but firm.

"Of course the girl can go. She wants to, so why not let her?"

"BUT SHE NEVER HAS GONE ABOUT ALONE BEFORE."

"Then it's time she began. You'll make her into a half-wit if you go on coddling her. Besides, I want you to go over my pass-book this afternoon."

"MUST SOMEONE GO TO-DAY?"

"I've settled it. Don't harp on it any more."

At two o'clock, Euphemia came down from her room where she had made ready for the journey. She was wearing her newest clothes, and as she paused for a moment in a shaft of sunlight that came through the doorway of the dining-room, she seemed to glow with beauty. Margaret had never seen her look so lovely, and a wave of violent affection swept over her. Impulsively she went up to her, and embraced her.

"My darling Phemy, take care of yourself. Promise me you'll take care of yourself."

Euphemia smiled.

"You speak," she said, "as if I were going on a very long journey. What is it? You mustn't cry."

"Oh, my dear, why can't I come with you?"

"No. It's better I should go alone."

"You look so lovely."

"Do you think so? I wish I could be as I am now, for ever. If I could make time stand still, I should—but not yet. Something very wonderful is going to happen to me, Margaret. I know it."

Margaret brushed away her tears, and then taking her sister's hand, kissed the scarred fingers many times.

"Phemy, let me tell you now how much I love you, how sorry I am if ever—you remember the awful thing I did——"

"What thing?"

"When I—I can't say it."

"I don't remember anything at all like that. I must go, Maggie. To-morrow I may have a surprise for you."

She freed herself gently from the embrace, and went to the door.

"Phemy, do promise that if your bed isn't properly aired you'll go to Stuart's, or even to a hotel."

Euphemia smiled.

"Of course I will. Good-bye—till to-morrow."

She got into the motor.

"When I come back," she continued, "I'm going to make one of those aquariums that we saw in the glass shop in Knightsbridge. I shall buy the bowl on my way to the station tomorrow. So if you see any pretty pebbles, transparent ones if you can find them, do save them for me, won't you? It'll be something for you to do this afternoon. Good-bye again."

She waved, and the chauffeur drove the car clumsily through the narrow gate.

"Hector would have gone through much more neatly," Margaret thought, as she turned sadly away and walked through the sloping garden to the sea.

B

The hot sun glared through the window of the railway carriage, illuminating a pattern of stains and points of dirt in the woodwork opposite.

Euphemia looked up from her book.

"The speed of light," she thought, "is 186,000 miles a second. The sun's light takes five minutes to reach us. So the sun is— 55,800,000 miles away. But it isn't. It's over 90,000,000 miles away. Perhaps it's 286,000 miles a second. Three sixes eighteen. . . . That's nearer. . . ."

She took out a piece of paper and a pencil, and made calculations. Then she turned the paper over and gazed exultantly at a mass of figures—her roulette statistics—with which the back was covered.

11. 8263 times.

19. 8244 times.

23. 8120 times.

35. 7969 times.

What about 7? 7642 times. How it had dropped behind. It was thoroughly beaten. Yet, when they first went to Shoreston it kept turning up and repeating almost every tenth spin of the ball, its gloomy message—"Gone away, gone away". Of course, it was August now, soon after Bank Holiday—a time when people left London. But the number hadn't turned up more than a dozen times during the last two days. Besides, shooting doesn't begin till the twelfth. He would have gone away for the Bank Holiday, and then come back for a night or two, to see to his affairs, before going up to Scotland. The numbers did not lie. It became clearer and clearer that they didn't. As for 35, Perella's number, it was altogether routed. No danger from her. She had gone to Frinton with her horrible baby and Lady Maule. Perella was out of the way.

Of course, her own health wasn't very good. There was no getting over 23. It never did very well, never reached the hundred first, but it was never very far behind. But 11, the beautiful and gracious number, the symbol of perfection and comfort, and love. Why should she not say it? Not the solitary unrequited love expressed by 2, but love answered, love burning in two bodies. How cunningly it had worsted all the others, Perella, absence, danger, ill-health, death, cross-purposes.

11. 8263 times.

Eight and two, ten, and six, sixteen, and three nineteen! Nineteen, the number of sudden calamity.

But that was pure superstition. How could the momentary total of the figures in a number mean anything at all? That afternoon, perhaps, she could try a few more spins—not too many, but just enough to pass that remote danger. How lucky that she had brought the wheel with her. Or had she forgotten?

With trembling hands, she dragged her suitcase from the rack and opened it. The little wheel was safely there, the ball still resting in the groove of 11. She lifted it out, put it on the seat beside her, and looked at it, her eyes full of desire. Five minutes passed, and she gave the wheel a spin.

C

Archibald and 'Genia lived in Durham Square, between the Park and Paddington. Though Mr. Moxhay had told Euphemia to warn them of her visit, she had forgotten to do so, and no one was prepared for her coming. As she was shown through the hall, she passed two doctors, one of them Dr. Miard, who attended to Mr. Moxhay. A nurse in uniform looked over the banisters, ran downstairs, spoke a hurried word to a scared servant, and ran upstairs again. On the landings above, doors opened and shut restlessly.

The house was very hot, and the blinds of the drawing-room, in which Euphemia waited, were drawn almost fully down to keep out the sunlight. Margaret, if she had been there, would have noticed the furniture and decorations, which were in the style of an Oxford Street shop window. She would have been sickened by the shining curtains of pale mauve brocade, the fat gilt tassels hanging from the fat silk cushions, the high polish of the "period" reproductions, the festoons of lilac that climbed on the expensive wall paper, the vastness of the sofas, the absence of book-cases. She would have compared the room, which summed up cruelly the taste of 'Genia and her three daughters, with the faded Victorianism of the house in Adelaide Square, the wilful neglect of all elegance shown by Rosa at Haybrook, Perella's bedroom on the Riviera, and the starved gentility of the house at Shoreston.

But Euphemia walked round the stuffy room deep in her own thoughts, wondering only from time to time when she would be able to go—as if, simply by being in the house and seeing no one, she were fulfilling her errand.

At length 'Genia came in, big, tear-stained, but not altogether unhappy, and after a vague greeting explained hurriedly that Archibald had had a bad attack that afternoon. Three minutes later she made excuses and went out, promising to send Phoebe in, if she could be found. Soon afterwards young Archibald put his handsome head through the doorway, withdrew it hurriedly, and then, remembering his manners, came in for a few words. He did not trouble to hide his grievance at being kept in London in August.

"God knows," he said, "how long we're to go on like this."

"But couldn't your father be moved?" Euphemia asked, recalling a phrase of Margaret's. "He would be so much better by the sea in this heat."

"They say they daren't move him just now. I'll see if I can find Phoebe. She went out to lunch, but she ought to be back by now. Pearl is somewhere about, too."

"And where's Jenny?"

"She and her baby and Cyril are in Devonshire, staying with old Mrs. Clark. We wired to them an hour ago. I don't know if they'll come back. They can't do any good. How's grandfather?"

"Oh, very well, thank you."

"Well, I'll go and look for Phoebe," he said, and went out quickly, leaving the door open. From time to time Euphemia heard hushed but agitated voices, and the nervous opening and shutting of doors.

Then 'Genia came in again.

"You must forgive us neglecting you like this. Where's Archie? Oh, Phoebe. I simply can't think where she's got to. I've sent Pearl to bed—the poor girl was so hysterical. The heat, really, I think. Well, dear Phemy, it's a very, very sad day for you to call. But won't you have some tea? What have they been thinking of? Do, just a cup. I'll have one with you. I need something. . . . And how is your dear father? I'm afraid, Phemy, you must tell him—if you think it wise—that the doctors are not happy about Archibald. Perhaps Stuart should tell him, though so far we haven't cared to say too much to Stuart. Winifred is such a talker, you know. . . . Some tea, please, Joyce. Just a little bread and butter and some cakes. . . . You know the Clarks are all in Devonshire. We've wired to them. Cyril's keeping closely in touch with the business. There's no need for your father to feel worried about that. You'll be sure to tell him, won't you? He has a report from the works manager three times a week, and he'll be back himself very soon. They all need a holiday so much though. Are you spending the night at Stuart's? Of course, it is inconvenient living in a suburb. Excuse me a moment. . . ."

When she came in again, the maid had laid the tea.

"Well, dear Phemy, you must tell your father—if you think it wise—or perhaps I'd better write to Margaret. You see, till this afternoon, no one had any idea that it was really so. . . . Poor dear Archibald, we can only pray and trust. I think Dr. Miard will be writing to Stuart, if he doesn't see him to-day or to-morrow. Perhaps we ought to have rung up Stuart this afternoon, but Winifred—you know what she is. Oh, must you go? Phoebe would have loved to see you. I can't think what the girl's doing. Archie shall see you home. Yes, it will be something for him to do, poor boy. . . . No trouble at all, but if you'd rather——"

Euphemia promised to call again the next morning, and escaped—unmoved and oblivious of all the messages.

She walked across the Park to Adelaide Square, and went straight to her bedroom, and looked out of the window. The windows of the house opposite were wide open, and the curtains drawn back. She could see, on a table, a whisky decanter, a siphon and two glasses. A sporting gun rested against the wall near the door. "As I knew," she murmured, "he is here."

She took off her hat, washed and changed her dress, singing to herself, and watching the window. There was no movement in the room which she had under observation, and in the end, she went down to the drawing-room.

In her honour the Joneses had removed most of the dust-sheets, though it was some time since the windows had been opened. Euphemia opened them, and let in a flood of scorching air from the street. She loved great heat, even though it usually made her pale and listless. It was one of those rare days, which make us forget that we live on a small island absurdly near the north pole, bring us into harmony with a foreign scheme of things, broaden our ideas and give them a continental, even a world-wide flavour. "Perhaps," Euphemia thought, "it is the last hot day of summer. He will be going in a few days to Scotland, where it's always misty and wet, with clouds rolling down the spiky hills, and drip, drip, drip, from the sodden branches. But to-night, it will be quite different. We might be in Africa, or Mexico, or one of those Pacific Islands. . . ."

Idly she opened the bureau by the window, and found an open book lying face downwards on the blotter. It seemed to her to have crept there like a forlorn little mouse seeking shelter, and she felt a moment's pity as she took it up.

"which becomes faith. Lay not therefore too hard a hold on these external things. For as no flame (save the true flame) can burn without destroying, so these things may not enter into your life without impairing it, corroding the veins through which the truth shall flow one day.

"O Joy conceived in darkness, and struggling to be born!

"O Joy . . ."

She put the book down on the piano meaning to take it up later to Margaret's room.

After supper, of which she did not eat much, she went back to her bedroom, and taking a manuscript book from a locked drawer, sat down near the window, and read, as the light failed.

The first entry was over two years old.

"Why am I writing this? Because I want always to feel what I am feeling now. I want my life to be different from everyone else's—

Margaret's, Archibald's, Stuart's, Hector's, Mortimer's. I am two people—one whom my family see, and another, a secret person living on a secret. . . .

.   .   .   .   .

"To-day I met him coming out of No. 18. It was about 4.45. I suppose he was going to his club.

.   .   .   .   .

"To-day I met him again, in Brinton Gardens. I dropped a parcel I was carrying, and he would have picked it up for me. But I picked it up myself, in case he should recognise me at the window. I know I shall meet him properly when the right time comes.

.   .   .   .   .

"I have found out his name, and his club. He is in *Who's Who*.

.   .   .   .   .

"Dr. Miard thinks my illness is a feverish chill. He does not know that X.'s aunt has left him a legacy, and that I am terrified he may move to a larger flat somewhere else. If he went, I couldn't stay on here.

.   .   .   .   .

"Is it possible to love anyone so much, to no purpose? I seem to be giving out an enormous force, which wastes away in the air. If it were turned to some other object, what couldn't it do? If faith can remove mountains, love could create them. I had to see the doctor again, and he looked down his nose and hummed and hawed. If they try to send me to Switzerland, I shall jump out of the window.

.   .   .   .   .

"I am not unhappy like Margaret, because I have an interest

in life. I wrote X four anonymous letters, but tore them up. We shall come together by spiritual means, and I almost regret having troubled to find out so much about him. I intend not to watch him from the window again.

.   .   .   .   .

"Resolution broken. Christmas and the awful crowd. Pestered by Margaret.

.   .   .   .   .

"Maggie is dead, and Margaret has gone to the funeral. About 12 the sun came through the fog, and showed me X sitting in his dressing-gown, by the chess-board. A problem, I suppose. His hair shone in the light. A very happy day."

.   .   .   .   .

The record rambled on for pages and pages, now simple and childlike, and now couched in phrases of theological grandeur, while at intervals came the monotonous question (to which the answer was alternately "Yes" and "No"), "Is it possible to love so much, to no purpose?"

The last entry, which she read by the last gleams of the daylight, was as follows:

"To-morrow we are going to captivity in Babylon. I shall not take this to Shoreston, as when we come back here, I know I shall want to find some link with the past waiting for me, even if (as, of course, I fear continually), X has gone away. It will have been something—and I believe in the truth of this, as I write it—to have been eaten up with this devotion to him. It will not all be wasted. Even if I have hurt others by it, as my 'strange coldness' hurts and frightens Margaret, it is no less a real and lovely thing."

She got up, and put the manuscript away, and then, wrapping

herself in a dark dressing-gown, so that no one should see her by
the window, took up her post again. There was no moon, but as
she waited the stars became brighter, and the air still warmer. A
heavy scent rose from some flowers in the depths of the courtyard,
and seemed to turn the dim irregular space into a garden full of
lurking surprise.

A clock struck ten. Then suddenly a light flashed on in the room
opposite, and the man with fair hair came to the window and
peered out. For Euphemia time stood still. Then the man pulled
the curtains together, leaving, in his careless way, a chink between
them of about three inches. There was a pause. Then he spoke,
and though Euphemia could not catch the words, she knew that
he was not alone.

As if in answer to a protest, the ramshackle curtain over the skylight twitched, and twitched again. There was a crash, and it fell to
the floor, revealing the whole room, the man standing and holding
a tangled cord, and by his side a young woman, bold, common
and pretty. Her voice rang vulgarly across the courtyard, while
his, suave and thick, seemed to reassure her. Then he dragged her
to the sofa, and sat beside her, putting his arm round her shoulder. With his other hand he offered her a glass of *crème de menthe*,
which was standing on a footstool. She sipped and spilt some of
the drink over his shirt-front. He took the glass from her, slapped
her playfully, and seized her in his arms. Cries, laughter, kisses—
and the love-scene began.

D

Euphemia did not sleep during the night. Next morning, her
memory told her that she must wash and dress, and she did so.
She could not eat. Her train for Shoreston left Charing Cross at
a quarter-past eleven. She reached the station soon after ten, and
then remembered, as if recalling an incident from childhood, that
she had intended to buy a glass aquarium in Knightsbridge. She
walked to Leicester Square and got into the tube. Opposite to her

was a young woman, bold, common and pretty. The flesh-coloured stockings on her fat legs showed big round stains of dirt or hair. As Euphemia gazed at her with horrified contemplation, the jaunty oval of the face, the red and pouting smile, the deliberate jutting of the breasts became familiar. It was she, the worm, the destroyer, the loathsome thing. Euphemia clenched her hands, while a torrent of anger swept over her, and her lips muttered abuse and menaces.

"I'll slit your nostrils for you, you filthy slut. Do you think your body pleases men? *Your* body? You haven't even washed your arm-pits. I'll have your teeth out. I'll run a red-hot iron round your lips. That'll redden them. What's your fee? Sixpence? Ninepence when you can get it? But, of course, you pick pockets as well, and blackmail. Do you really expect men to pay you, when you look like that? To pay, for touching your diseased skin?"

Unperturbed, and ignorant of her offence, the young woman tapped the floor with her flimsy little shoe, hummed, and peered gaily round at the men in the carriage. At Hyde Park Corner, she got out, and Euphemia, oblivious of everything but her hatred and the new imperious need to outrage her mortal enemy, followed closely behind. In the lift, they stood side by side. At the top, the woman stepped nimbly off the pavement, and darted across the road. Euphemia hesitated for a moment, and then, a beautiful and absurd figure, waving her parasol, gave reckless chase. Half-way across the street, an omnibus knocked her down, and there was no Lord Kithen at hand to lose his life for hers.

The dead body was taken to St. George's Hospital, and identified by means of an envelope. The caretaker at Adelaide Square telephoned to Stuart, who was the first of the family to hear the news.

X

SEPTEMBER

HECTOR had motored to Shoreston. He arrived purposely at the hour of Mr. Moxhay's rest, as an excuse for not seeing him. He found Margaret by the edge of the cliff, at the bottom of the garden. It was early in September, and the calm surface of the sea was streaked with the furrow of a little pleasure-yacht.

It was the first time he had seen Margaret since Euphemia's death; for she had been so overcome by the news that the doctor would not let her go to the funeral. Her ill-cut black dress made her seem even paler than she was.

"I have come to take you for a holiday," he said, when they had greeted. "We must get a nurse for our father. It's no use saying you can't leave him. You must, or you'll get too run down to be of any use to him later."

She looked at him blankly.

"I'm as well here as I can be anywhere. It'll be all right till we have to go back to Adelaide Square."

"Nonsense, you need a change from this dismal place."

"I don't find it dismal. I'm very fond of it."

"It has so many memories, I suppose," he said savagely. "It's so full of your self-sacrifice that you find it easy to go on being the maid of all work. It won't do. You're becoming plain and dull. You're spoiling yourself, and I can't bear to see it. You're the only one in our awful family with any character, the only one of any real value, the only one with anything to give other people, and I won't have you dried up—like a fountain lapped up at the source by horrible mouths. Do you miss her so much?"

"Hector——"

"Don't try to force me into shirking things. I've come to smash these barriers. I know the old trouble between her and you, and all the responsibilities you forced on yourself and even the absurd story of——"

"Oh, Hector, don't——"

They were climbing down the rough steps in the rock. As she spoke, she swayed with faintness and clutched his arm.

"My poor, dear girl. Come and sit beside me on this uncomfortable shingle, and listen to me. I'm bad at leading up to things gently and you must forgive my clumsiness, but I'm going on."

"Not yet—not now——"

"Now. I know your silly secret, and the absurd story of two bad-tempered little girls who quarrelled by the nursery fire, years and years—too many years—ago. Let me tell you a story. There was a boy at my school who was very home-sick. His bed was next to mine in the dormitory, and I could hear him crying every night under the bed-clothes. I don't know why—a kind of devil seemed to possess me—or perhaps it was only a natural healthy cruelty of which I have a good share—I longed to make him really miserable, and it was a kind of game to see how I could torment him. I used to twist his wrists, pull his hair and do all the things to him that bullies do to small boys. He used to tremble when he saw me approaching him. But that wasn't enough. He developed a fantastic sort of affection for me, and though he used to cry and struggle, I could see he didn't really mind the physical pain I gave him. So in the end, I pretended I'd stolen a letter from his mother. I found an envelope in the waste-paper basket addressed to him in her writing—small boys can ferret out everything—and used to dangle it in front of him. That did hurt him. It was an ingenious and loathsome form of cruelty for which I should have been horse-whipped. Before the end of term he was taken away and sent to a sanatorium. He was consumptive. We heard that he didn't live very long."

Margaret stared at the sea, and said nothing.

"And what does it all amount to?" he went on. "What difference does it make now, that thirty years ago a small boy, whose body has somehow turned into mine—a wretched little brat whose existence I deplore—behaved like a cad?"

"It was her birthday," Margaret said after a pause. "I had given her a horrid imitation coral necklace which she didn't like. I tried to make her wear it, and she wouldn't. The string broke and the beads ran all over the floor. I dragged her to the fire and took her hand——"

"I know, I know."

"I pressed her fingers against the hot bar. She screamed, but I held her there—it was the left hand end of the lowest bar—there was a huge lump of red coal just above——"

"What were they doing, to leave children in a room with a fire and no guard?"

"There was a guard, but I pulled it off. I held her fingers just underneath the red hot coal, and counted, 'One, two, three, four' —oh, Hector——"

She turned over on her face, while her tears streamed among the pebbles. A deep explosion at Midhampton quarry shook the air and the beach. It was half-past three.

"Next week," Hector said, "I'm arranging for Rosa to divorce me."

Margaret raised her head.

"From that day, you know, she was never the same."

"That," he almost shouted, "is damned nonsense. Even as a baby she was—strange. She was always, ever since I can remember her crawling on the floor, awkward and obstinate. This diary that Stuart found——"

"What diary?"

"Oh, he was too shocked to tell you, perhaps. She had an absurd infatuation for one of your neighbours. She used to spy on him from her window. It's not uncommon. These repressed women— don't think I'm referring to you, you ministering angel——"

"You realise, Hector," she asked in a flat voice, "that I shall always think I killed her?"

"That accident? How many people, is it, are run over in London every day?"

"Did she mention me in the diary?"

"Only casually, and selfishly. She knew you were worried about her, and said she couldn't help it if you were."

They were both silent, while a venturesome rowing-boat from Shoreston passed in front of them. Inside it, a young woman kept shouting, "For Gawd's sake, let's get back to the pier before Ernie gets there." Overhead two big seagulls chased one another in circles. Hector lay on his back and watched them.

"There was a tag in Virgil I used to like," he murmured, "something about *degere vitam more ferae nec tales tangere curas*—I've got it wrong. 'Live for the moment, like an animal.' Why aren't we enjoying this air and sun, quietly and calmly? Why do we remember and anticipate? Why is the past more real than the present? Why can't we say, 'Here we are, sitting happily by the sea,' and leave it at that?"

"Because——" Margaret answered.

"Oh, don't bother to think of the reasons why we can't."

"Hector, about this divorce of yours?"

"That's settled. Rosa, I think, will marry again."

"And you?"

"Oh, I'm not made for marrying. I shall fly about from place to place, free and detached, like those birds."

"There are two of them."

"When I am lonely enough, I shall be driven to make friends."

"If father knew——"

"My dear Maggie, you've practised facing horrible absurdities for so long that you can surely face a little unpleasantness during the next few months. Father will be furious, at first. He won't like it, either, if John becomes a Roman Catholic, as he threatens to do. His friend, Kenrick, the organist he's been learning from, has just been converted, and I'm afraid it's inevitable. But I shan't be banished for ever. His disapproval doesn't count with me."

"Is it impossible for you to wait?"

"What, five or ten years, at my age? They are too precious. Look how poor Archibald has waited. Do you suppose he has been contented and happy?"

"I think so. He loves his family, and hasn't a discontented nature."

"Perhaps. We're different. You know, Maggie, he's very ill indeed? You must face that, too."

"But Dr. Miard wrote, only a week ago——"

"I saw him the day before yesterday, when I called at Archibald's. He wasn't reassuring."

She put her handkerchief to her eyes.

"The same evening," he said after a pause, "I met Kithen at the club. He asked after you."

"He's a nice man."

"I think so. He has improved a good deal. Have you decided what you would do if he asked you to marry him?"

"How could I leave father now?"

"Easily. He would be delighted at the match. He would engage a dozen nurses rather than prevent it. Wouldn't he?"

"Yes."

"Over this, you must make no mistake."

"But there's Perella."

"I shouldn't be surprised if Kithen prefers you. It's rather funny really. She introduced him to you so as to give you a taste of her *monde*, hoping to dazzle you—I've no illusions left about that woman. Besides, she wouldn't dare to marry him while our father is alive, in case he should think she was cutting you out—unless, of course, you refused him definitely."

For the first time Margaret took the initiative in the conversation.

"Haven't I heard you say," she asked, "that she was irresistible?"

"Yes, perhaps. Irresistible and worthless. Kithen should be saved from that."

"Hector, did you at all——?"

"Which of two questions is it now?"

"Have you never been in love with Perella?"

She blushed as she spoke, and looked away from him.

"Fascinated, yes, but never in love."

"I was afraid of it," she muttered, "and hated her for not being good enough for you."

He dug his fingers into the shingle and flung a handful in the air.

"You might," he said, "have been going to ask me about Kithen

—if I said anything important to him, or if he said anything important to me."

"Oh, I'm not curious about him. Besides, he'll meet all kinds of women now."

"Well, we shall see. Only I beg this of you—do what you want, and not what others want."

He looked at her, and she looked back and smiled.

"Let us sit here," he said, "for five minutes and think of nothing."

They sat, listening to the little waves fumbling at the wet and sandy slope that was now the margin of the sea, smelling the seaweed drying on the rocks, and watching the rowing-boat as it went back towards the town, the circling gulls and far above them the wisps of white that streaked the blue.

"What are you thinking of?" asked Hector suddenly.

"Winter in Adelaide Square."

That evening, after Hector had gone, and she had said good night to her father, she sat in her bedroom and watched the sea again. The violence of her feelings during the first part of her talk with Hector on the beach had left her in a mood of almost rapturous lassitude—the mood of serene acquiescence in the outward beauties of the world which she used to have as a girl during her first walk in spring after a bad cold, a delicious blending of bodily weakness and spiritual calm. The cares of a life-time and the agonies of the past month seemed suddenly to have slipped from her shoulders like a heavy cloak, leaving her frail but free. Whether she had been right to be tormented, whether the peace would soon be broken by another storm, did not disturb her.

A breeze had risen and fair weather was less sure. But the sea was still calm. In the distance, a large boat ablaze with lights crossed the bay. Margaret took it to be a private yacht, and idly pictured to herself the dancers behind the striped awnings, and the lively little band whose music seemed to reach her ears in fitful bursts of rhythm between the stirrings of the sea. The whole air, indeed, was full of musical phrases, echoes from works which she had idealised before she had come to know them too well, vague memories of works once heard and then almost forgotten, and other sounds, now sombre, now crisp and gay, tangled together like silk threads on the wrong side of a piece of embroidery. And as the boat became smaller, and its many lights converged, it seemed as if even the bay had changed, and she had before her a stretch of unknown water, through which she herself were at last cruising for pleasure, while an unknown coast on the horizon encircled her like an attractive dream.

But when she had fallen asleep by the window and begun to dream, she was again on the Shoreston promenade. It was empty except for one beggar, a decrepit and grimy little man, wearing a battered bowler hat and holding out his hand for alms. As she hurried past, he reminded her of someone she knew. "If he is starving, as his placard says," she thought, as she walked on, "I should have given him something. Why was I so mean?" The thought troubled her, and she had to recall all the stories about the prosperity of beggars—how they are a limited company in which the most deformed and pitiful are the biggest shareholders—in order to soothe her conscience. "If he is still there when I come back," she decided, "I will give him a shilling."

She reached the end of the promenade, walked round the newspaper kiosk, which was shut, and began the return journey. The beggar was still in his place by the deserted entrance to the pier. As she passed him she fumbled with her bag, but somehow the moment was over before she could find the money, and she felt too self-conscious to turn round. Then, when she had nearly reached the other end of the promenade, she was ashamed of her embarrassment. "Must he go hungry," she thought, "because I am too shy to give him anything? There is no one else about to-day who can help him. I must go back." And she went back, trying to make her gait seem purposeless, as if these comings and goings had no connexion with the lonely man who watched her with pathetic eyes. In passing him the third time she had noticed his eyes, and realised that had it not been for the clothes he might have been

Alec Kithen. She was now clutching the shilling in her gloved fingers, and decided at all costs to give it to him the next time she saw him.

Once more she walked round the newspaper kiosk and set out for home. In the distance, the man was still standing by the entrance to the pier. As she approached him her steps became slower, and sometimes she stopped walking altogether and looked at the sea, in the hope that he would lose heart and leave his pitch before she reached it. But he did not go, and she was forced with trembling hand to put the shilling into his, which trembled too.

He did not thank her, but when she had walked barely twenty yards beyond him he suddenly called out, "Lady! Lady!" She looked round, filled with dismay, and afraid that he might pursue her. He did not move, however, and after a long moment of indecision, she went back to him herself, defiantly, and yet knowing that it was to be no ordinary encounter.

He looked at her—it was not Alec Kithen—and then said huskily, "It's a bad shilling." He held it out in his dirty palm, and she saw at once that he spoke the truth. The coin was pitted and cut, and bore no resemblance at all to any piece of English money. Once more her callousness and her fear gave way to shame.

"Oh, I am so sorry," she said, as she ransacked her bag. "I can't think how I made such a mistake."

"I didn't think," he said, "that you'd give me a bad shilling when you needn't have given me anything at all."

Suddenly it occurred to her that he was trying to cheat her, and had substituted another coin for hers.

"That's not the shilling I gave you."

He looked at her with his large blue eyes, and said nothing. He was more like Hector than Alec Kithen.

"It was a proper English shilling I gave you," she continued, almost pertly so as to hide her agitation. "You're trying to trick me, aren't you? It's no use. You've got my shilling, haven't you?"

He said nothing, yet she couldn't walk away and leave him.

"Yes or no?"

"Yes."

The answer came miserably and pitifully. But it was she who blushed and felt ashamed.

"Why had you to do that?" she asked gently.

"Can you spare nothing more?"

In her bag, she could only find a ten-shilling note. She took it out, and he looked at it greedily.

"This is all I have, I'm afraid. If you have any change——"

"I only have a shilling—your shilling."

They looked at one another in silence. "After all," she thought, "could I afford it, just this once? Is it so great a folly?"

"Take it," she said at length.

He hesitated for a moment.

"Can you really spare it?" he asked.

"Yes, I can spare it quite well. It's more than I should really afford, of course, but——"

The inadequacy of her words to express what she felt was heart-rending. Tears came into her eyes, and also, surprisingly, into his.

"I need it so much," he said, looking at her as if he could not let her go. The bell at Cliff House sounded for luncheon, and she knew that it would take her forty minutes to reach home. Still she hesitated. For once they could wait for her.

"I have nothing more."

"Then," he said slowly, changing his shape and becoming bigger and more powerful, "let me kiss your hand."

She laughed nervously.

"This is absurd."

"Give me your hand."

"Leave me alone."

As she spoke, he took her hand in his, unbuttoned her glove, pulled it off gently, and dropped it on the promenade. She had no thought of resisting.

"I need your strength."

"Take it."

For a moment he held her hand, then, turning the sleeve back carefully, he placed the bared wrist against his lips. She could feel the bristles of his moustache pricking her skin.

"Your strength," he seemed to mutter, "and your blood."

Suddenly knowing what was to happen, she bowed her head in acquiescence. He opened his lips, and, after licking her wrist with his tongue, he caught the skin between his teeth, and bit. She felt one stab of violent pain, and then, shutting her eyes and reeling, she sank into a dizzy ecstasy, while her blood gushed from the wound, wetting his mouth and chin and frayed grey collar, and her whole being seemed to pour out with it, deliciously leaving the body that once had been hers.

XI

OCTOBER

ALEC KITHEN called at Cliff House at a quarter to one. As he approached, forcing a way through the relentless gale, he saw Margaret pacing up and down at the end of the garden, by the rocks. Without ringing he walked round the house and joined her.

It had been a morning of alarms. At breakfast came a letter from Stuart, with the gravest news of Archibald. Stuart had also written in a more hopeful vein to Mr. Moxhay, who, however, with his usual shrewdness, had asked Margaret whether she had received a letter too. In spite of her attempts at subterfuge, he drew the truth from her, read her letter, and became so agitated that she had to send for the local doctor. He was in any event coming at eleven that morning to meet Dr. Miard and Dr. Frost, who were visiting another case in the neighbourhood. They had arranged to call on Mr. Moxhay with a view to persuading him to go back to London and consult yet another doctor. This doctor, a Dutchman named Desiderius, specialised in an obscure and very modern operation, which they hoped might prolong Mr. Moxhay's life another twenty years.

So the doctors came and talked, and Mr. Moxhay, infected with their optimism, agreed to return to Adelaide Square as soon as possible. Even long-standing deafness, they said, was not beyond the Dutch doctor's range. They went at half-past twelve, and Mr. Moxhay, fatigued with the excitement, fell asleep. Watts, who now slept in a little room next to his, was within call.

It was wet and stormy. An endless procession of swollen clouds raced over the house, while the sea drenched the garden wall with spray.

"Margaret!"

She wore an oilskin coat and no hat, and her hair glistened with foam and rain.

"You, Alec! To-day!"

"Am I so tender a plant?"

He had almost to shout, the wind was so strong.

"Come in," she said, "though——"

He divined that for some reason she did not wish to go in.

"If we could get out of the gale," he suggested, "and talk for a moment——"

"We could shelter behind the rock, if you don't mind going down."

From the window, Watts was watching them. Margaret looked up at him and pointed downwards, so that he should know where to find her if she were needed. Since the day of Euphemia's death, when she had found him wiping his red eyes in the pantry, she had ceased to dislike him. He nodded to show he understood.

Kithen followed, as she led nimbly down to the shelter—the leeward side of a boulder which lay diagonally to the main mass of the rock.

Briefly she told him of the morning's events. His own excitement was so great that he could hardly spare the time to express his sympathy.

"May I now talk to you about myself?" he asked. "Or is it, I wonder, too foolish a time?"

There was something in his exhilaration to which she felt herself respond.

"Talk," she said. "Say anything."

"I love you."

She knew that he was in earnest, and almost understood how the long struggle with his own ineffectualness had suddenly brought about a crisis of romance, in which he might embark on any folly with a light heart.

She said nothing, and he seized her wrist and kissed it, like a baby playing with a toy. She wondered what to say, and nearly asked him where his motor was.

"I have thought about you perpetually," he said. "The less I see of you, the more I think of you. It is the real test. Or isn't it? Anyhow, I am here. I couldn't come sooner. You have known, too, for some time. It's not sudden. Will you marry me?"

"No."

("How many times," she asked herself, "shall I have to say this, to convince him?")

He paused for a long time, looking at her, while the radiance left him and old habits of thought, polite, self-critical and kind, possessed his mind once more.

"Just 'No'?" he said, with a poor smile.

"Not marriage, or my love—all my affection. Oh, my dear, I am so sorry. We can do least for those who are kindest to us."

"Then, there is someone else. No, it doesn't follow. You're not being faithful, Margaret, to that friend you lost in the War?"

"No, I promise you. I have almost forgotten him."

"Then who stands between us?"

He had to continue his questions, however foolish, or go away, and this he could not bring himself to do.

"No one," she answered. "Don't ask me to explain, because one can't explain these things—to oneself even. I am not made for love. The joy of life—the ordinary joy of life—has missed me, some-how. You have loved women before, and will love others."

"If they have gossiped about me——," he said angrily.

"No, it's not that. I have heard no gossip. If I loved you, your previous——"

(Was it to be "amours", "adventures" or "love-affairs"? A wretch-ed sentence to have begun.)

"Not loving me, you can't be jealous even of what I haven't done, you mean?"

"If you must say it so cruelly."

"I have lived really a quiet and timid life, basking in my brother's reflected glory. I have pretended, of course—but the more I explain myself, the more worthless you will think me."

"Marry Perella!"

He recoiled.

"What you want," she continued, speaking very quickly, "is

some charming woman, full of animal spirits, never moody, capricious or introspective—someone who will push you forward, shut her eyes to your faults, if you have any, and by her zest for life make life real for you, in the way you have imagined it—a healthy full-blooded woman who has seen things and done things, and only longs to see and do more—my opposite. But why should I enumerate her attractions? You have felt them yourself."

He said nothing.

"I know you have. When my father dies, she will inherit Mortimer's share—as much as any of us will get. She would be very glad to marry you. And my father will be glad too."

"Would your father dislike your marrying me?"

"No."

"I thought perhaps it was out of regard for him——"

"No."

Her volubility had suddenly failed. The only sentence now in her head was "Marry Perella and keep her from Hector," but she was already ashamed at her brazen advocacy of Perella's merits, and began inwardly to reproach herself for not having sent him away before.

"This talk of Perella," he said querulously, "is too absurd. It is as wrong for you to suppose that if I can't marry you I can marry her as it is for me to suppose that if you won't marry me it must be because you have someone else in mind. It's become terribly like a farce—and I go on talking——"

She looked at her watch.

"Come and see me again—in London. My answer will be the same, but I don't want to lose you altogether."

She moved out into the wind, and they scrambled up the rock together.

"The Royal Banana is closed," he found himself shouting. "You remember our drive?"

"Yes, yes."

She walked round to the gate with him.

"Where is your motor?" she asked.

"In Shoreston, being decarbonised. The walk will do me good."

Were there tears in his eyes, or was it the rain?

"Good-bye."

He began to apologise for coming, for staying, for his impetuosity and crudeness, but she cut him short.

"Not now. If you come to London, we can meet as soon as you like. Good-bye. Good-bye."

The gate shut, and he raced down the road, a buoyant little figure in his mackintosh. The serio-comic interlude was over.

Mr. Moxhay was very talkative that afternoon. The prospect of a complete cure at the hands of the Dutch doctor elated him, and he was full of the details of the homeward journey. He had forgotten Archibald's illness and Euphemia's death. He had not, however, forgotten Kithen's visit, reported to him by Watts, and it was not long before he touched upon it.

"So you'll be sorry to go from here, will you? Well, if I were younger, I dare say I should like it better than London. Perhaps I shall, another year, when I've seen the Dutchman. What was his name?"

She took up the slate.

"Dr. Desiderius."

"What's the first letter?"

"D."

"I thought so. I wish you could write better. You make your Ds like Ps. Put another twenty years on my life, they said. Well, it may be, it may be. So you don't want to go back to London?"

"I don't like winter much."

"A bit dull for you, I dare say. Will put twenty years on my life. That's good news, isn't it, Maggie? Isn't that good news?"

"You know how glad I am to hear it."

"Twenty years! Why, twenty years ago, I was—I was only a young man. Did I hear you had a caller this morning?"

She nodded.

"Who was it?"

"Alec Kithen."

"*Lord* Kithen?"

She nodded.

"And what had he to say to you, I wonder. Mind, Maggie, there are times for plain speaking, and I'm going to speak plainly. If that young man asks you to marry him, you'll do well to say 'Yes.' I shall expect you to say 'Yes.' I want to see all my children comfortably settled before—though if they're right about this Dutchman that won't be for a long time. Still, I've no doubt I could find a bit to settle on you now. You can have Hector's share. He's been an ungrateful son. Now this Lord Kithen—coming here on a day like this, he must have had something in view. Has he spoken of his intentions at all?"

He looked at her suddenly, with brutal directness. The pencil trembled in her hand.

"I TOLD HIM WE WERE GOING BACK TO LONDON——"

"What's that? Your writing gets worse every day. That's not what I asked you. Answer my question. Has he given you to suppose what his intentions are?"

She nodded, desperately.

"He has? Do you mean—for God's sake, child, give me a straight answer—he has asked you to marry him?"

She nodded.

"This morning?"

She nodded.

"And you told me nothing about it? What did you say to him? What was your answer? Quick——"

"I TOLD HIM I COULD NOT MARRY HIM."

"Are you a fool? Think, Margaret, think. I don't want to be hard on you, but this—this is intolerable! Here is a young man you like and admire, a young man of good appearance and good family. . . . My poor girl, what have you to hope for, if you throw away chances like this? Answer me, at once. What have you to hope for?"

"I DON'T KNOW."

"Nothing, I tell you. Nothing. You're—what is it?—twenty-eight now——"

"36."

"Thirty-six! Do you want to spend all your time sitting alone

in Adelaide Square, an old maid? Where are your wits? *I* don't
need you. You know that. You're useless to me—you clumsy and
careless fool. Any nurse in London is worth a dozen of you. I don't
want you here. I don't want you in the house. What possessed you
to refuse him?"

She sat still, and wrote nothing.

His rage was so great, he almost struck her.

"Answer me. I order you to answer."

"I DON'T LOVE HIM, FATHER. AND PLEASE, DEAR FATHER, BE CALM
AND SPARE ME A LITTLE——"

She gave him the slate, and covered her burning cheeks with
her hands.

Once more, she sat in her room. She had made countless arrangements, telephoned for the ambulance which was to take her
father to London, telephoned to Adelaide Square, sent two of the
servants ahead to make preparations, countermanded orders to the
local tradesmen and asked for their books, written to the house-
agent to send a care-taker to Cliff House, which they were leaving
three weeks before the tenancy expired, written a line of sympathy to 'Genia, written to Stuart. She was numb and exhausted. The
rain beat on the window, and bubbled up busily inside the sill. It
seemed hardly possible that it was here she had seen so many radi-
ant mornings, spent so many hours watching the quiet sea and
the dark arm of the bay; that below the same garden wall was the
sunlit beach on which she had strolled and bathed, and gathered
transparent stones for Euphemia, and sat and talked with Hector
about him and herself; that here she had spent the summer which
now was over.

They were going back in two days to Adelaide Square, to the
house of long windows curtained with green plush, to the fogs
and the cold, and Euphemia's empty room. More visits from
Stuart, more dutiful calls from the Clarks, tearful messages from
'Genia, the telephone, the telephone, and the shadow of another
Christmas, Winifred's hymns, Perella—and no Euphemia. "My
children, my grand-children, my great-grandchildren . . . a year

ago, dear Mortimer was with us. And now my son, my eldest son Archibald. . . ."

She wept, for Archibald and herself. He was so good and so kind—not with the brutal kindness of Hector, who could change her world with a smile from grey to rose—but with a steady little glow of gentleness which had been precious to her. Yet she knew in her heart that it was an irrelevant grief. He was wrapped up in his wife and his children. This was their tragedy, not hers. She felt about it as she would feel if she heard of a calamity which befell the dear friend of a friend.

There were other troubles nearer at hand: the crisis she would have to meet over Hector, his divorce, his son's change of religion, his exclusion from the family, her father's anger at her rejection of a good marriage, the care of him during his operation or treatment, the querulous solicitude of her relations, their suggestions, their reproofs, their pity. Try as she would, she, who had made it the habit of a life-time never to let her actions be determined by her own misery or joy, could no longer keep her personal wretchedness from mingling with more legitimate emotions. She had lamented for Euphemia and Archibald—this was allowed, but the time had come when at last she lamented for herself.

Weakly, she opened her blotter and began to write:

"MY DEAR ALEC—If you can bring yourself to marry me, without love on my side—if what you said this morning was not said in a moment of excitement of which you already feel ashamed. . . ."

She put down her pen, and looked at the letter with scorn. How could he say, so soon afterwards, that he had yielded to an access of folly, even if it were so? And it might even be so, probably was so, without his knowing it. This sudden impulse of his to marriage had a thousand possible reasons—weariness of his home life, the pricking of his bachelor conscience, the obligation to perpetuate the barony, a revulsion from some woman who had behaved badly to him. Was marriage with love on neither side conceivable? Yet why not?

"Here is escape," a voice whispered. "Here is your one loophole.

Your father wishes it. You like the man. Even should he not love you, he will always be good to you. And with your training, it will be easy for you to be a good wife to him. Why hesitate any longer? Be wise in time!"

In a few lines she finished the letter, sealed it and addressed the envelope. "This," she found herself saying, "is good-bye," and while she sat with her eyes wandering from the blotter to the dripping window-sill and the creaking Venetian blind, she was filled with a sense of irrevocable farewell. It was not that her past life rose up with a spurious charm, gilding a "girlhood's innocence", and making it seem a bliss too great to part with. The contrary, rather, was true. The humiliations and bitter memories of years stood in her way, reminding her of the dark strength with which she had borne them, the discipline with which she had fettered and braced herself, and below all, the sombre purpose, image or romance—there was no word for that elusive aspiration—of which, in the worst days even, she had seldom been unaware.

Despite her follies and failures there had been, in the core of the long deliberate martyrdom, nothing vain or aimless, nothing unworthy or mean, no hint of destiny without an ultimate grandeur. And it was *this*—this most real part of herself and her inner life—to which, in a moment's weariness of the flesh, she was being disloyal. She was betraying strength for weakness, endurance for ease, the far for the near. The treachery was too great, too fatally simple, too unpardonable.

She tore the letter in small pieces, pulled up the blind and got into bed. The rain beat against the shaking window and the whole house swayed, while a siren hooting at the coast-guard station told of a wreck at sea.

XII

NOVEMBER

A

It was six weeks after the return to Adelaide Square. Dr. Desiderius had not yet performed his famous operation, but held out hopes of it if all went well. He had, in the meanwhile, been treating Mr. Moxhay with new medicines, which invigorated the patient but made him excitable and more than usually despotic. Archibald's doctors had twice changed their diagnosis, but were unable to give him much relief. They decided, however, that there was a treatment to be obtained in Germany which might do him good, and he was sent off to the *Kurort* with his wife and Phoebe. Mr. Moxhay was interested in no illness save his own, but was alarmed to think that his business was now in the sole charge of Cyril Clark. He insisted that both Archibald's son and Stuart's eldest son, Eric, should dispense with further education and begin straightway to serve their apprenticeship at the works. Archibald was too ill to protest, and Stuart had no wish to do so. Margaret was continually busy. She was, if not the centre of the family, the means of its communications. Alec Kithen had called twice. Both visits had been colourless and unsuccessful. He was ashamed of his behaviour at Shoreston, and she was too preoccupied to re-establish a more quiescent friendship. Besides, the house in Adelaide Square, which in its brightest days had seemed fit only for family reunions, was more than usually unpropitious as a meeting-place. He asked her to go out with him, but she refused. She had many harsh words from her father on this score, till by a lucky chance she was led into suggesting that the match would be a good one for Perella. Mr. Moxhay, who in many ways preferred Perella to his own daughters, was more than a little pleased with the project, and let fall such hints of settlements that it became clear that Perella, when the opportunity came, would show none of Margaret's reluctance to take it. Alec, disappointed in Margaret, shy and rather lonely, turned to Perella once more, and the whole family was confident that at least one of Mr. Moxhay's grand-daughters would have a peer as her stepfather. This was Margaret's only relief from gloom.

There remained Hector and his affairs—his separation and divorce from Rosa, and his acquiescence in his son's conversion to the Roman Church and abandonment of all serious work for a musical career. Mr. Moxhay's feelings towards him were complex. He disliked him more than any of his children, for his financial independence and aloofness from the family. At the same time, these odious qualities gave him a prestige which none of the others enjoyed, and Mr. Moxhay began to credit him with abilities which he may not have possessed, and to believe that if only he could be persuaded to replace Archibald in the business it might regain its old prosperity. For this reason, when Stuart, whose sense of duty always came perilously near to tale-bearing, made some unfavourable but vague comments on Hector's way of life, Mr. Moxhay was slow to seek greater precision of detail, in the hope that if he turned a blind eye to whatever it was that Stuart intended him to see, Hector might once more draw near to the fold, and play the part of a dutiful son. Once caught and bound by a contract, he could be bullied and humbled. Margaret saw the casting of the net, and hardly knew what to pray for. It was unbearable to think that Hector should be harried and put upon as Archibald had been, but even more unbearable to think of his perpetual banishment from the house and an embargo on further intercourse with him. She was uncertain both how much Stuart knew, and how much her father had been told, but she had some experience of Stuart's gift for discovering the truth when it was ugly.

In the end, the inevitable happened. Mr. Moxhay grew tired of waiting for Hector to approach him with an offer, and Stuart, who had by now learnt the full story of John's apostasy and Hector's divorce, could keep the knowledge to himself no longer, and in a long but lucid letter to his father set out the hideous facts.

It was a great tribute to the treatment of the Dutch doctor, that Mr. Moxhay's fury did not kill him as soon as he heard the news.

B

It was a quarter to four when Hector reached Adelaide Square. He had received his father's urgent telegram that morning at Haybrook, where he was seeing to the dismantling of the house. He well knew the nature of what it portended, and would have disregarded it if he had not had a painful and despairing letter from Archibald, who was terrified that his death would leave his wife and children unprovided for. He would be content, he wrote, if a quarter of the income he had received as managing director could be capitalised and settled on Eugenia and his children. It was more than he could bear to have worked in the business at a good salary for so many years, and to die unable to support the home he had built up. Hector, in spite of all his efforts to be unmoved, could not ignore the appeal, in which the very triteness of the phrases, taken, as they seemed to be, from a letter written in the middle of the last century, emphasised the writer's agony and fear. This trouble, coming in the middle of his own troubles and transcending them, threw him into an unusual agitation; for he knew that he could only plead Archibald's cause successfully by surrendering his own freedom, and throughout the journey he had to nerve himself to make the distasteful sacrifice.

For a long while, he had rehearsed his opening speech, the different arguments which he would use, the evasions with which he would parry the attack. He had imagined, as he thought, all the insults with which he could be met and devised soft answers to them. He had pictured the beginning and the end, a handshake or a blow. Whatever happened he must be calm.

As he rang the bell, he trembled.

He was shown into the empty drawing-room, where he had not been since Christmas of the year before. As he paced up and down, waiting for his father, who preferred seeing him there to in his bedroom, all the familiar objects in the room seemed to sap his strength of will and leave him defenceless to the coming onslaught. Nothing had changed. The green plush curtains hung in thick folds by the windows, framing the fog. The picture of the Grand Canal was still tilted. Each of the many ornaments on the mantel-piece was rigidly in its old position, as if glued to the marble. In front of the alcove the wooden negress supported the same palm. The same heavy ivory paper-knife lay diagonally on the whatnot at the end of the sofa. Hector picked it up, and played with it, remembering a Sunday evening years ago when he had been cutting the pages of a French novel with it and had been suddenly forbidden both to use that paper-knife and to waste his time reading filthy trash in the drawing-room. So, he thought, might Margaret gaze at a corner of the fireplace in the old nursery, and remember the exact spot where she had held the mad Euphemia's fingers to the bar. One should change one's furniture every year, before it could build up associations against one.

He walked again to the two windows facing the square. Not even the pavement was visible in the fog, which grew thicker every moment. On the writing-table between the windows was a book, *The Conflict of the Soul*, by Shamus O'Geoghegan. He remembered having seen it about the room at Christmas time. As always, it opened at page 103.

"which becomes faith. Lay not therefore too hard a hold on these external things. For as no flame (save the true flame) can burn without destroying, so these things may not enter into your life without impairing it, corroding the veins through which the truth shall flow one day.
    "O Joy conceived in darkness and struggling to be born!
    "O Joy. . . ."

The door opened, and Mr. Moxhay came in, supported by Watts. He gave Hector no sign of recognition till he was seated on the sofa and Watts had left the room.

C

"See that the door is shut."

Hector obeyed.

"Sit there, and take the slate."

Hector took it from the whatnot, where Watts had left it, and read a sentence at the bottom in Margaret's writing, which was only half erased.

"PLEASE, FATHER, WOULD YOU MIND IF I WENT OUT FOR TEN MINUTES TO . . ." The rest was blank.

"Look at me!"

He looked up with a start, and saw the big face, swollen and blotched above the white and wiry hair which covered cheeks and chin.

"I sent for you because I wish to ask you some serious questions, questions so serious that I could never have believed that a day would come when I should have to ask them of any son of mine."

The resonant voice hummed with emotion.

Hector made a sign for grace and wrote busily.

"PLEASE GIVE ME ONE MOMENT. I THINK I KNOW WHAT YOUR QUESTIONS ARE, AND I AM AFRAID DISCUSSION OF THEM WILL BE PAINFUL. BUT FIRST, BEFORE WE TALK OF MY AFFAIRS, I DO WANT TO GIVE YOU A MESSAGE FROM ARCHIBALD, WHO IS SO SERIOUSLY ILL."

"What does Archibald want? Don't play for time with me! My doctor is coming in half an hour."

"ARCHIBALD HAS ASKED ME TO ASK YOU IF YOU COULD POSSIBLY SETTLE SOMETHING ON EUGENIA AND THE CHILDREN. AS YOU KNOW, HE HAS NO CAPITAL TO LEAVE THEM, AND IT WOULD GIVE HIM GREAT PEACE OF MIND IF HE COULD FEEL ASSURED THAT THEIR FUTURE———"

"Give me that rigmarole."

Hector passed him the slate. After all, what more could he add? It was hard to appeal for pity in block capitals. Mr. Moxhay read the message slowly.

"I know. I know. Like the rest of you he wants my money before I'm gone. How do I know what I shall want myself yet? I shall live for another twenty years, the doctors tell me. Let him wait a bit."

Hector snatched the slate.

"HASN'T HE WAITED NEARLY——" he began, then erased the sentence, and substituted, "HE WANTS NOTHING WHILE HE'S ALIVE. HE MAY BE DEAD IN A FEW WEEKS, AND IF YOU WISH HIM ANY HAPPINESS, YOU WILL——"

"Give me the slate. . . . That's my affair. My money's my affair. Who asked you to meddle with this matter?"

The question was so obviously answered that Hector did not interrupt.

"As for 'Genia and her children, I shall make what provision I think proper. Tell him that. Haven't I taken young—what's his name? —Archibald's son—what's his name?"

"ARCHIE."

"Haven't I taken him into my business? What more does he want?"

"I IMAGINE THE WAGE YOU ARE GIVING ARCHIE CAN HARDLY SUPPORT THE WHOLE FAM——"

"Stop scribbling and listen to me. You can tell Archibald this. If anything should happen to Archibald—and I sincerely trust it will not—I shall see that his family is not destitute. As for a settlement, it's quite impossible. Why, only yesterday, I settled Mortimer's share on Perella, in consideration of her marriage with—with— you know the man I mean. Am I to beggar myself while still alive and healthy? Why, I might outlive you all, even now. The doctors say I shall live another twenty years. . . ."

He paused, to set his thoughts in order, and then continued in an angrier tone.

"I sent for you, not to be badgered about settlements, but because I have some questions to ask you, which you will answer without equivocation. I am told that your wife is divorcing you. Is that so?"

Hector nodded.

"Then I say it shall not be! D'you hear me? It shall not be."

"It must. The case is down for trial."

"Do you mean to tell me that a son of mine has sunk so low—has picked up the habits of the gutter and disgraced the good name of an honourable family?"

He went on for some minutes, asking rhetorical questions, and working himself into an assumed passion—assumed, because at the back of his mind he knew the harm to be already done, and had resolved that the real struggle with his son should be over another matter, where redress was still possible. Hector made no reply. Neither the time nor the slate-pencil favoured a discussion of ethics. He only wondered whether he had done sufficient justice to Archibald's request.

"I am ashamed of you. And there is an even graver wrong, which you can still set right. What is your son doing?"

"He is studying music."

"Music! Where?"

"At present he is having lessons from the organist at Ramshott Church, but I hope in a month or two——"

"Give it to me. What sort of a fellow is this organist?"

"I am told he is a very competent musician, worthy of a better job."

"That's not what I asked you. Is he a strict disciplinarian? Has he a good moral influence on your son?"

"I hope so. I have heard nothing against him."

"Is he a Roman Catholic?"

"Yes. He became one a few months ago."

"Has he any influence over your son's religious beliefs?"

"Perhaps. But I hope John is old enough to think things out for himself."

"Is it true that your son is in danger of becoming a Catholic?"

"I am afraid it is not unlikely."

"Afraid it is not unlikely! You sit there calmly and say that. Do you think any money of mine will go to a Roman Catholic? You must be mad. Where's your authority? Have you no mind of your own? Are you doing nothing to prevent such a wanton act of folly?"

"IT ISN'T A MATTER OVER WHICH I FEEL ENTITLED TO EXERCISE ANY AUTHORITY I MAY HAVE. I HOPE VERY MUCH THAT JOHN'S COMMON SENSE WILL HELP HIM TO SEE THROUGH THE SILLY BUSINESS. BUT IF IT DOESN'T——"

"Let me see that. What then?"

"I SUPPOSE HE'LL GO OVER."

"And what will you do?"

"NOTHING."

"Oh, so you'll do nothing, will you? And what do you suppose I shall do when I find a grandson of mine caught by that mumbo-jumbo? What shall I do, eh?"

"I THINK IF YOU ARE REASONABLE YOU WILL FEEL AS I DO."

"And do nothing, eh? Let him take his Peter's pence to the Scarlet Woman, eh? You're a fool, man. You're a fool."

The real passion had begun. They looked at one another with hatred for a moment, and Mr. Moxhay went on:

"I'll tell you what I'll do. First, I'll cut him and you clean out of my will. I'll consider your daughter's position later. But as for you and your boy, not a penny of my money will you get. Is that clear enough?"

Hector nodded.

"But that's not all. I disown you—both of you. I shall close this house to you, and my other children will do the same. I shall forbid you to see them or write to them. I shall forbid them to see you or write to you. I've had enough of you and your foul brood."

"BY WHAT RIGHT I WONDER," Hector began to write, but the squeaking of the pencil exasperated him beyond endurance. With an oath he flung the slate into the grate, where it broke into two or three pieces. Then he darted to the writing-table, where he found a writing-block in a drawer.

"HOW DARE YOU TRY TO CONTROL OTHER PEOPLE'S RELIGIOUS BELIEFS? WHAT DO YOU KNOW ABOUT RELIGION?"

Mr. Moxhay waved the block away, and continued:

"I give you one chance, which is more than many a father would give a son who acted as you have. This is it. You'll take your son away from his precious organist, and his rubbishy music and his creeping to the Cross, and you'll pack him neck and crop into my business. Eight hours a day, and no nonsense. He'll start level with young Archie and Eric. If he gives satisfaction, I shall treat him as I shall treat them. If he's no good, he can stay at the bottom of the ladder. As for you, you've had some business training, and I don't mind paying you a salary to work with Cyril Clark. If you both join us on these terms, I'm willing to overlook the past. Otherwise, I've done with you."

For one moment the foolish old man believed that Hector would accept the offer. The fire died in his eyes, and his expression became half appealing and half sly. Meanwhile, Hector was writing hurriedly.

"JOHN HAS AN APTITUDE FOR MUSIC AND NONE FOR YOUR BUSINESS. I SHOULD STRONGLY ADVISE HIM AGAINST WASTING HIS LIFE LIKE ARCHIE AND ERIC. AS FOR ME, YOU OUGHT TO KNOW BY NOW THAT I HAVEN'T THE SMALLEST INTENTION OF JOINING YOU. YOUR UNPARDONABLE TREATMENT OF ARCHIBALD DOESN'T ENCOURAGE ANYONE TO WASTE A LIFETIME IN YOUR SERVICE."

"Give that to me."

"I've not done, damn you!" Hector shouted, and making a gesture, he wrote on.

"IF YOU HAD ANY CONCEPTION OF THE MEANNESS OF YOUR TYRANNY OVER THE WHOLE FAMILY I THINK YOU WOULD BE ASHAMED."

"Oh, bother these capitals," he muttered, and breaking a rule established for a dozen years, continued in script:

"You've eaten up Archibald's life, and now you're going to eat up his son's and Eric's. As for poor Margaret, your behaviour to her is inexcusable. What right have you to live on keeping a whole family in subjection, interfering with the actions and thoughts of people who are in every way your superiors?"

The sheet came to an end. He passed it contemptuously to his father and began the next.

"What right have you to regulate their morals—you, with your Phari-

saical Victorian code? What right have you to dictate their religion—you, the least spiritual of men, a theological ignoramus?"

At this point there was a roar, and Mr. Moxhay, attempting feebly to rise, broke into an inconsequent tirade.

"You scum! You filth! Out of the house with you! Out of my house! So it has come to this, has it? You dare to teach your father a lesson, dare you? If I had a horsewhip, I'd show you who is master here! I'd break every bone in your body, you ungrateful lout, you dirty adulterer——"

Then Hector too lost control of himself. He threw the writing-pad aside, snatched the paper knife and stood up, making wild passes in the air, eager only to shout his father down.

"That's right," he yelled, "bully us all into the grave before you go there yourself! It won't do, I tell you, it won't do. It's you who need the horsewhip, and by God I'm going to give you a taste of it! Do you suppose I'm going to sit here quietly while you regulate my affairs, telling me what my son is to believe, telling me what's honourable and what isn't? I'm sick of you, do you hear, sick of your tantrums and your domineering. Why should we make martyrs of ourselves for the sake of your worm-ridden carcass? Why should a girl like Margaret, who might have been a lovely and charming creature, turn into a dotty old woman in order to keep you going? What use are you? Answer me! This time I'm going to play the bully. What use are you to anyone?"

He paused for breath, and looking down, saw his father, who sat terror-stricken while his lips moved inarticulately. Hector thought he was still shouting, and continued, this time with dangerous quietness:

"You see, you need a lesson, and I'm going to give it you. No, shut your mouth. Shut your mouth. You will please shut your mouth. I dislike talking to people who keep their mouths open. Will you shut your mouth, or shall I shut it for you?"

He made a few passes with the paper-knife in front of Mr. Moxhay's face, and then, seized with a sudden spasm of fury, struck the gaping lips with the flat of the ivory. Mr. Moxhay tottered for one moment and then crumpled up and fell sideways head first on to the brass fender.

There was a knock at the door, and Margaret came in.

D

"Hector! What has happened?"

Hector fell back into the arm-chair.

"I think I've killed him."

Without speaking she locked the door, and ran across the room to her father's huddled body.

"Help me to lift him. Quickly."

Together they laid the body on the sofa. Unhesitatingly Margaret ripped open her father's coat and shirt and felt for the heart.

"He's dead."

"Are you sure?"

"Yes."

"Then what are we to do?"

For the moment he felt detached from what had happened, though something told him that in another few seconds he would either shrug his shoulders and become himself, or break down.

"Hector, my dear, what happened?"

"We were having an argument, and both lost our tempers. I struck him on the mouth with that knife, and he fell down—like that."

She looked at her father's mouth. There was blood on the lips. She took a handkerchief and wiped them, and noticing that the false teeth were out of position, put them back.

"It was an accident," she said. "You see, there's a bruise on his chin where he hit that knob."

"I killed him."

Then with a sudden shudder, he flung himself on the floor by her side, broke into tears, and seized her hand. Gently she knelt down by him, and kissed his hair.

"Hector, my darling, don't cry. In a few minutes everything will be all right. He had to die, soon. It'll pass. It'll all pass. Don't cry, my darling."

For a while he clung to her so closely that she couldn't move.

"Margaret, promise me you'll never leave me. You'll never forsake me?"

"Never. I promise you."

She rose to her feet.

"The three doctors were to be here at half past four," she said. "I'd better telephone to Dr. Miard, though I think he'll have started."

"Margaret, will they know?"

"They were prepared for this. They must have been prepared for it."

"My finger-prints are on the paper-knife."

"What if they are?"

She took the knife and wiped both blade and handle carefully on her skirt. Then she fingered it herself.

"They're not there now. Mine are there instead."

"You mustn't do that!"

She smiled at him.

"After all, why shouldn't I touch a paper-knife in my own drawing-room?"

"Someone must have heard us shouting."

"I did. Nobody else."

"There's Watts."

"I sent him out as soon as he brought father in here, to get some medicine made up, and to do some other things as well. He won't be back for another quarter of an hour."

"What about the nurse?"

"She's in her room—Phemy's room, you know, at the back. She can't have heard anything there."

"Suppose someone saw, through the window?"

"What, in this fog? You can't even see the street lamp. Now, I must just telephone to Dr. Miard."

"The doctors will know."

"Not they! They're not looking for trouble. After all, we pay them. Besides, there's no trouble to find. You must go up to my room and lie down, while I telephone. I'll come up in one minute myself."

She led him to the door, unlocked it, and when they had gone through, locked it on the outside. Then she took Hector up to her room, settled him on an ottoman, and went downstairs to the telephone. Dr. Miard, she was told, had already set out for Adelaide Square. She went once more to the drawing-room, shut the door and looked round. Then she noticed the broken slate in the fireplace. She took the pieces and put them nearer where her father had fallen, erasing the words "BY WHAT RIGHT", which were still incriminatingly visible in one corner. She found also the sheet of paper which had brought about the final outburst, and the sheet on which Hector had been writing when it occurred. These she burnt, pressing them well into the heart of the blaze. Then, waiting quietly, she listened for the front-door bell.

The three doctors had come. She sent the maid away, and, hardly speaking, led the black procession to the drawing-room.

Then she said, "My father is dead. He had a seizure about twenty minutes ago. He is there—on the sofa."

Dr. Miard and Dr. Frost hurried across the long room to the body. Dr. Desiderius studied the picture of the Grand Canal.

Dr. Miard, the family doctor, was the first to speak.

"I am afraid it is true. My dear Miss Moxhay—I cannot tell you how grieved I am. Of course we feared such an eventuality, but there was no reason to anticipate——"

He took her hand and looked at Dr. Frost.

"No reason," said Dr. Frost, and sighed. "Of course, if we had been able to exercise more control——"

He looked at Dr. Desiderius, who was still looking at the Grand Canal.

"May I ask if you were present?" inquired Dr. Miard. "Was there —er—any agitation——?"

"I was here," she said, "with my brother Hector. We were discussing some family affairs—my father insisted upon it. I am afraid he did become agitated. It was a financial matter. . . ."

The two men nodded.

"In the middle of rather a heated sentence, my father fell forward and struck his face against the fender. There was nothing I could do. As you know, I understand a little nursing."

The doctors bowed and murmured.

Then Dr. Frost, Dr. Miard's senior partner and already half a specialist, stepped forward.

"My dear young lady, you know you have all my sympathy. Being present at so sudden an end has been a great strain upon you, and I see how bravely you are bearing it. In a sense we must look upon it as a merciful release; for although——"

He looked at Dr. Miard, who looked at Dr. Desiderius.

"Although," said Dr. Miard, "we had great hopes of effecting a considerable betterment both in the general condition and—er—in the special disability under which your father was labouring, until——"

"Until," Dr. Frost continued, "Dr. Desiderius had a more favourable reaction to the treatment, we had no assurance, though, of course, the probability was slight, that——"

He broke off and bowed gently to Dr. Desiderius, who approached the fire.

"Quat zo," said Dr. Desiderius.

There was a pause.

"Is your brother here?" asked Dr. Miard.

"Yes. I have made him lie down. He was very much distressed, and reproaches himself for having joined in the discussion. As for that, he had no choice. I think, being a stranger to the house, and my father's illness, he takes it more hardly than I. Do you need to see him?"

"Oh, no, not now."

"My brother Stuart will make all the arrangements."

"Quite."

"I will ask him to communicate with you."

"Thank you."

"There is, of course, no question of a post-mortem or an inquest?"

The English doctors looked at the Dutchman, who shook his head.

"Oh, no," said Dr. Frost.

"The cause of death," said Dr. Miard, "is only too apparent. And now perhaps——?"

"I will send Nurse down to you. Watts is out at present."

"Thank you so much."

"Good-bye."

She shook hands gravely with the three. Dr. Desiderius walked with her to the door, and opened it for her. In her last glimpse of his big bearded face, she thought she caught the vestige of a smile.

E

Since she had never set her heart upon material possessions, it was easy for her to realise that in a few days she would leave Adelaide Square for ever, easy for her to become, as it were, disembodied and walk like a powerful spirit freed from the unwanted flesh boldly towards the unfamiliar. The seeds of courage, long planted in her, bore sudden fruit, and filled her at last with such strength that she could almost have wished for greater trials over which to exercise it. Such things as she had to do were all too simple.

First she telephoned to Stuart, who was appalled, and broke into reproaches.

"If I had been there," he said, "this would not have happened. You have neglected him. You have not prayed enough."

She answered him kindly, and only begged him not to try to come to the house that night. Apart from his cold, it would, she said, be almost impossible for him to find his way in the fog. Besides, Hector was there.

Then she went to her bedroom and talked to Hector. He was lying as if paralysed on the ottoman, aching in every limb, and hardly able to speak.

"It is too much for me," he said at length. "I shall go to the police station, and give myself up. Why must it be to me that this has happened? It is like an accident, in which one suddenly loses one's arms and eyes."

"Nothing has happened to you."

"You were not there. If you had been, I should never. . . . Why couldn't you have been there? That was when I needed you!"

"You need me now, and I am free and able to look after you. The past is over. That is the miracle."

"Margaret, you must never leave me again."

"I promise you."

At supper she ate a little, and coaxed him to eat.

"Is Stuart coming to-night?" he asked.

"I did all I could to stop him."

"If he comes, what shall I do?"

"You shall not see him."

"I can see no one, except you."

"You needn't."

He got up and went to the window.

"Margaret, I'm going out. I can't be here if Stuart comes. The fog's not quite so thick. I'm going now."

"Very well, I'll come with you."

"But if he comes?"

"We shall be out, that's all."

"What will he think?"

"Oh, that we've both gone mad."

They walked round the square, turned into Pont Street, and then out of it. It was like a walk in a dream, noiseless and effortless and of immeasurable distance. The fog grew thick again and swirled round them, so that unconsciously they would often pause and feel for the next step.

"Margaret."

"Yes."

"I thought I had lost you. Give me your hand."

"Here it is."

"What shall we do?"

"When? Now—or later?"

"Now. Shall we go back?"

"Are you tired?"

"No. Are you?"

"Not at all."

"What did you mean when you said, 'Now, or later?'"

"I wondered for a minute where you would want to go—in a day or two—to-morrow—any time."

"Where can we go?"

"Anywhere, except to the Poles. Africa, or the South Seas, or Littlehampton."

"And leave all this behind—and build things up—on the old foundations again?"

"The old foundations are buried. We are being born now. The world is waiting for us, like a piece of blank paper, on which we can write as we choose."

They walked on a long way in silence.

"Margaret, do you know where we are?"

"No—but it doesn't matter."

THE END

ALSO AVAILABLE FROM VALANCOURT BOOKS

Michael Arlen	Hell! said the Duchess
R. C. Ashby (Ruby Ferguson)	He Arrived at Dusk
Frank Baker	The Birds
Walter Baxter	Look Down in Mercy
Charles Beaumont	The Hunger and Other Stories
David Benedictus	The Fourth of June
Paul Binding	Harmonica's Bridegroom
Charles Birkin	The Smell of Evil
John Blackburn	A Scent of New-Mown Hay
	Broken Boy
	Blue Octavo
	A Ring of Roses
	Children of the Night
	The Flame and the Wind
	Nothing but the Night
	Bury Him Darkly
	Our Lady of Pain
	Devil Daddy
	The Face of the Lion
	The Cyclops Goblet
	A Beastly Business
Thomas Blackburn	A Clip of Steel
	The Feast of the Wolf
John Braine	Room at the Top
	The Vodi
	Life at the Top
Jack Cady	The Well
Michael Campbell	Lord Dismiss Us
R. Chetwynd-Hayes	The Monster Club
	Looking for Something to Suck
Isabel Colegate	The Blackmailer
Basil Copper	The Great White Space
	Necropolis
	The House of the Wolf
Hunter Davies	Body Charge
Jennifer Dawson	The Ha-Ha
Frank De Felitta	The Entity
A. E. Ellis	The Rack
Barry England	Figures in a Landscape
Ronald Fraser	Flower Phantoms
Gillian Freeman	The Liberty Man
	The Leather Boys
	The Leader

RODNEY GARLAND	The Heart in Exile
STEPHEN GILBERT	The Landslide
	Monkeyface
	The Burnaby Experiments
	Ratman's Notebooks
MARTYN GOFF	The Plaster Fabric
	The Youngest Director
F. L. GREEN	Odd Man Out
STEPHEN GREGORY	The Cormorant
ALEX HAMILTON	Beam of Malice
JOHN HAMPSON	Saturday Night at the Greyhound
ERNEST G. HENHAM	Tenebrae
	The Feast of Bacchus
THOMAS HINDE	The Day the Call Came
CLAUDE HOUGHTON	Neighbours
	I Am Jonathan Scrivener
	This Was Ivor Trent
JAMES KENNAWAY	The Mind Benders
	The Cost of Living Like This
CYRIL KERSH	The Aggravations of Minnie Ashe
GERALD KERSH	Clock Without Hands
	Neither Man Nor Dog
	The Great Wash
	On an Odd Note
	Fowlers End
	Nightshade and Damnations
FRANCIS KING	To the Dark Tower
	Never Again
	An Air That Kills
	The Dividing Stream
	The Dark Glasses
	The Man on the Rock
C.H.B. KITCHIN	Birthday Party
	Ten Pollitt Place
	The Book of Life
	A Short Walk in Williams Park
HILDA LEWIS	The Witch and the Priest
JOHN LODWICK	Brother Death
GABRIEL MARLOWE	I Am Your Brother
KENNETH MARTIN	Aubade
	Waiting for the Sky to Fall
MICHAEL NELSON	Knock or Ring
	A Room in Chelsea Square
BEVERLEY NICHOLS	Crazy Pavements
OLIVER ONIONS	The Hand of Kornelius Voyt

DENNIS PARRY	The Survivor
	Sea of Glass
J.B. PRIESTLEY	Benighted
	The Doomsday Men
	The Other Place
	The Magicians
	Saturn Over the Water
	The Thirty-First of June
	The Shapes of Sleep
	Salt Is Leaving
PETER PRINCE	Play Things
PIERS PAUL READ	Monk Dawson
FORREST REID	Following Darkness
	The Spring Song
	Brian Westby
	The Tom Barber Trilogy
	Denis Bracknel
ANDREW SINCLAIR	The Facts in the Case of E.A. Poe
	The Raker
DAVID STOREY	Radcliffe
	Pasmore
	Saville
RUSSELL THORNDIKE	The Slype
	The Master of the Macabre
JOHN WAIN	Hurry on Down
	Strike the Father Dead
	The Smaller Sky
	A Winter in the Hills
HUGH WALPOLE	The Killer and the Slain
KEITH WATERHOUSE	There is a Happy Land
	Billy Liar
	Jubb
	Billy Liar on the Moon
COLIN WILSON	Ritual in the Dark
	Man Without a Shadow
	The World of Violence
	Necessary Doubt
	The Glass Cage
	The Philosopher's Stone
	The God of the Labyrinth

CPSIA information can be obtained
at www.ICGtesting.com
Printed in the USA
FFHW020713280319
51208025-56691FF